AMERICA

OR,

LAND, LAKE, AND RIVER

BY

Nathaniel Parker Willis

VOL. I

PREFACE.

Either Nature has wrought with a bolder hand in America, or the effect of long continued cultivation on scenery, as exemplified in Europe, is greater than is usually supposed. Certain it is that the rivers, the forests, the unshorn mountain-sides and unbridged chasms of that vast country, are of a character peculiar to America alone—a lavish and large-featured sublimity, (if we may so express it,) quite dissimilar to the picturesque of all other countries.

To compare the sublime of the Western Continent with the sublime of Switzerland—the vales and rivers, lakes and waterfalls, of the New World with those of the Old—to note their differences, and admire or appreciate each by contrast with the other, was a privilege hitherto confined to the far-wandering traveller. In the class of works, of which this is a specimen, however, that enviable enjoyment is brought to the fire-side of the home-keeping and secluded as well; and, sitting by the social hearth, those whose lot is domestic and retired, can, with small cost, lay side by side upon the evening table the wild scenery of America, and the bold passes of the Alps—the leafy Susquehanna with its rude raft, and the palace-gemmed Bosphorus with its slender caïque. So great a gratification is seldom enjoyed at so little cost and pains.

In the Letter-press, it has been the Writer's aim to assemble as much as possible of that part of American story which history has not yet found leisure to put into form, and which romance and poetry have not yet appropriated—the legendary traditions and anecdotes, events of the trying times of the Revolution, Indian history, &c. &c. It is confidently hoped, that the attempt to assemble a mass of interesting matter under this design, has not failed; and that, in the value of the intellectual portion, as well as in the beauty and finish of the embellishments, the Work will be thought worthy of the patronage of the public.

THE North Eastern Part OF THE UNITED STATES.

AMERICAN SCENERY.

It strikes the European traveller, at the first burst of the scenery of America on his eye, that the New World of Columbus is also a new world from the hand of the Creator. In comparison with the old countries of Europe, the vegetation is so wondrously lavish, the outlines and minor features struck out with so bold a freshness, and the lakes and rivers so even in their fulness and flow, yet so vast and powerful, that he may well imagine it an Eden newly sprung from the ocean. The Minerva-like birth of the republic of the United States, its sudden rise to independence, wealth, and power, and its continued and marvellous increase in population and prosperity, strike him with the same surprise, and leave the same impression of a new scale of existence, and a fresher and faster law of growth and accomplishment. The interest, with regard to both the natural and civilized features of America, has very much increased within a few years; and travellers, who have exhausted the unchanging countries of Europe, now turn their steps in great numbers to the novel scenery, and ever-shifting aspects of this.

The picturesque views of the United States suggest a train of thought directly opposite to that of similar objects of interest in other lands. There, the soul and centre of attraction in every picture is some ruin of the past. The wandering artist avoids every thing that is modern, and selects his point of view so as to bring prominently into his sketch, the castle, or the cathedral, which history or antiquity has hallowed. The traveller visits each spot in the same spirit—ridding himself, as far as possible, of common and present associations, to feed his mind on the historical and legendary. The objects and habits of reflection in both traveller and artist undergo in America a direct revolution. He who journeys here, if he would not have the eternal succession of lovely natural objects—

"Lie like a load on the weary eye,"

must feed his imagination on the future. The American does so. His mind, as he tracks the broad rivers of his own country, is perpetually reaching forward. Instead of looking through a valley, which has presented the same aspect for hundreds of years—in which live lords and tenants, whose hearths have been surrounded by the same names through ages of tranquil descent, and whose fields have never changed landmark or mode of culture since the memory of man, he sees a valley laden down like a harvest waggon with a virgin vegetation, untrodden and luxuriant; and his first thought is of the villages that will soon sparkle on the hill-sides, the axes that will ring from the woodlands, and the mills, bridges, canals, and rail-roads, that will span and border the stream that now runs through sedge and wild-flowers. The towns he passes through on his route are not recognizable by prints done by artists long ago dead, with houses of low-browed architecture, and immemorial trees; but a town which has perhaps doubled its inhabitants and dwellings since he last saw it, and will again double them before he returns. Instead of inquiring into its antiquity, he sits over the fire with his paper and pencil, and calculates what the population will be in ten years, how far they will spread, what the value of the neighbouring land will become, and whether the stock of some canal or rail-road that seems more visionary than Symmes's expedition to the centre of the earth, will, in consequence, be a good investment. He looks upon all external objects as exponents of the future. In Europe they are only exponents of the past.

There is a field for the artist in this country (of which this publication reaps almost the first-fruits) which surpasses every other in richness of picturesque. The great difficulty at present is, where to choose. Every mile upon the rivers, every hollow in the landscape, every turn in the innumerable mountain streams, arrests the painter's eye, and offers him some untouched and peculiar variety of an exhaustless nature. It is in river scenery, however, that America excels all other lands: and here the artist's labour is not, as in Europe, to embellish and idealise the reality; he finds it difficult to come up to it. How represent the excessive richness of the foliage! How draw the vanishing lines which mark the swells in the forest-ground, the round heaps of the chestnut-tops, the greener belts through the wilderness which betray the wanderings of the water-courses! How give in so small a space the evasive swiftness of the rapid, the terrific plunge of the precipice, or the airy wheel of the eagle, as his diminished form shoots off from the sharp line of the summit, and cuts a circle on the sky!

The general architecture of the United States cannot pretend, of course, to vie with that of older countries; yet, taken in connexion with the beautiful position of the towns, no drawing will be found deficient in beauty, while many of the public buildings especially are, as works of art, well worthy the draughtman's notice. The curiosity now generally excited with regard to this country, by its own progress, and by the late numerous books of travels, will throw a sufficient interest around every point that the pencil could present.

——"The green land of groves, the beautiful waste,
Nurse of full streams, and lifter up of proud
Sky-mingling mountains that o'erlook the cloud.
Erewhile, where yon gay spires their brightness rear,
Trees waved, and the brown hunter's shouts were loud
Amid the forest; and the bounding deer
Fled at the glancing plume, and the gaunt wolf yell'd near.
    "And where his willing waves yon bright blue bay
Sends up, to kiss his decorated brim,
And cradles, in his soft embrace, the gay
Young group of grassy islands born of him,

2

And, crowding nigh, or in the distance dim,
Lifts the white throng of sails, that bear or bring
The commerce of the world;—with tawny limb,
And belt and beads in sunlight glistening,
The savage urged his skiff like wild bird on the wing.

* * * * * * * * * *

"Look now abroad—another race has fill'd
These populous borders—wide the wood recedes,
And towns shoot up, and fertile realms are till'd;
The land is full of harvests and green meads;
Streams numberless, that many a fountain feeds,
Shine, disembower'd, and give to sun and breeze
Their virgin waters; the full region leads
New colonies forth, that toward the western seas
Spread, like a rapid flame, among the autumnal trees.

* * * * * * * * * *

"But thou, my country, thou shalt never fall,
But with thy children—thy maternal care,
Thy lavish love, thy blessing shower'd on all—
These are thy fetters—seas and stormy air
Are the wide barrier of thy borders, where
Among thy gallant sons that guard thee well,
Thou laugh'st at enemies: who shall then declare
The date of thy deep-founded strength, or tell
How happy, in thy lap, the sons of men shall dwell."—Bryant.

NIAGARA FALLS, FROM THE FERRY.

The best way to approach Niagara is to come up on the American shore, and cross at the ferry. The descent of about two hundred feet by the staircase, brings the traveller directly under the shoulder and edge of the American fall—the most imposing scene, for a single object, that he will ever have witnessed. The long column of sparkling water seems, as he stands near it, to descend to an immeasurable depth, and the bright sea-green curve above has the appearance of being let into the sky. The tremendous power of the Fall, as well as the height, realizes here his utmost expectations. He descends to the water's edge, and embarks in a ferry-boat, which tosses like an egg-shell on the heaving and convulsed water; and in a minute or two he finds himself in the face of the vast line of the Falls, and sees with surprise that he has expended his fullest admiration and astonishment upon a mere thread of Niagara—the thousandth part of its wondrous volume and grandeur. From the point where he crosses, to Table Rock, the line of the Falls is measurable at three quarters of a mile; and it is this immense extent which, more than any other feature, takes the traveller by surprise. The tide at the Ferry sets very strongly down, and the athletic men who are employed here, keep the boat up against it with difficulty. Arrived near the opposite landing, however, there is a slight counter-current, and the large rocks near the shore serve as a breakwater, behind which the boat runs smoothly to her moorings.

It may be remarked, that the well-known stanzas on the "Fall of Terni," in the fourth canto of "Childe Harold," are, in many respects, singularly and powerfully descriptive of Niagara.

> "The roar of waters!—from the headlong height
> Velino cleaves the wave-worn precipice;
> The fall of waters! rapid as the light
> The flashing mass foams shaking the abyss;
> The hell of waters! where they howl and hiss,
> And boil in endless torture; while the sweat
> Of their great agony, wrung out from this
> Their Phlegethon, curls round the rocks of jet
> That gird the gulf around, in pitiless horror set,
>
> "And mounts in spray the skies, and thence again
> Returns in an unceasing shower, which round,
> With its unemptied cloud of gentle rain,
> Is an eternal April to the ground,
> Making it all one emerald:—how profound
> The gulph! and how the giant element
> From rock to rock leaps with delirious bound,
> Crushing the cliffs, which, downward worn and rent
> With his fierce footsteps, yield in chasms a fearful vent,
>
> "To the broad column which rolls on, and shows
> More like the fountain of an infant sea
> Torn from the womb of mountains by the throes
> Of a new world, than only thus to be
> Parent of rivers, which flow gushingly,
> With many windings through the vale:—Look back
> Lo! where it comes like an eternity,
> As if to sweep down all things in its track,
> Charming the eye with dread,—a matchless cataract,
>
> "Horribly beautiful! but on the verge,
> From side to side, beneath the glittering morn,
> An Iris sits, amidst the infernal surge,
> Like Hope upon a death-bed, and, unworn
> Its steady dyes, while all around is torn
> By the distracted waters, bears serene
> Its brilliant hues with all their beams unshorn:
> Resembling, 'mid the torture of the scene,
> Love watching Madness with unalterable mien."—Byron.

VIEW FROM WEST POINT.

Of the river scenery of America, the Hudson, at West Point, is doubtless the boldest and most beautiful. This powerful river writhes through the highlands in abrupt curves, reminding one, when the tide runs strongly down, of Laocoon in the enlacing folds of the serpent. The different spurs of mountain ranges which meet here, abut upon the river in bold precipices from five to fifteen hundred feet from the water's edge; the foliage hangs to them, from base to summit, with the tenacity and bright verdure of moss; and the stream below, deprived of the slant lights which brighten its depths elsewhere, flows on

4

with a sombre and dark green shadow in its bosom, as if frowning at the narrow gorge into which its broad-breasted waters are driven.

Back from the bluff of West Point extends a natural platform of near half a mile square, high, level, and beautifully amphitheatred with wood and rock. This is the site of the Military Academy, and a splendid natural parade. When the tents of the summer camp are shining on the field—the flag, with its blood-bright stripes, waving against the foliage of the hills—the trumpet echoing from bluff to bluff, and the compact batallion cutting its trim line across the greensward—there are few more fairy spots in this working-day world.

On the extreme edge of the summit, overlooking the river, stands a marble shaft, pointing like a bright finger to glory, the tomb of the soldier and patriot Kosciusko. The military colleges and other buildings skirt the parade on the side of the mountain; and forward, toward the river, on the western edge, stands a spacious hotel, from the verandahs of which the traveller gets a view through the highlands, that he remembers till he dies. Right up before him, with the smooth curve of an eagle's ascent, rises the "old cro' nest" of the culprit Fay, a bright green mountain, that thrusts its topmost pine into the sky; the Donderbarrak, or (if it is not sacrilege to translate so fine a name for a mountain,) the Thunder-chamber, heaves its round shoulder beyond; back from the opposite shore, as if it recoiled from these, leans the bold cliff of Breknock; and then looking out, as if from a cavern, into the sunlight, the eye drops beyond upon a sheet of wide-spreading water, with an emerald island in its bosom; the white buildings of Newburgh creeping back to the plains beyond, and in the far, far distance, the wavy and blue line of the Kattskills, as if it were the dim-seen edge of an outer horizon.

The passage through the highlands at West Point still bears the old name of Wey-gat, or Wind-gate; and one of the prettiest moving dioramas conceivable, is the working through the gorge of the myriad sailing-craft of the river. The sloops which ply upon the Hudson, by the way, are remarkable for their picturesque beauty, and for the enormous quantity of sail they carry on in all weathers; and nothing is more beautiful than the little fleets of from six to a dozen, all tacking or scudding together, like so many white sea-birds on the wing. Up they come, with a dashing breeze, under Anthony's Nose, and the Sugar-Loaf, and giving the rocky toe of West Point a wide berth, all down helm, and round into the bay; when—just as the peak of Crow Nest slides its shadow over the mainsail—slap comes the wind aback, and the whole fleet is in a flutter. The channel is narrow and serpentine, the wind baffling, and small room to beat; but the little craft are worked merrily and well; and dodging about, as if to escape some invisible imp in the air, they gain point after point, till at last they get the Donderbarrak behind them, and fall once more into the regular current of the wind.

TRENTON FALLS.
(VIEW DOWN THE RAVINE.)
Trenton Falls (called Cayoharie by the Indians) are formed by the descent of a considerable stream, known by the name of West Canada Creek, through a mountainous ravine of singular formation and beauty. The Creek, which is swollen to a tremendous torrent by rains in the mountains, or by the spring thaws, has evidently worn through the strata which now enclose it, and runs at present over a succession of flat platforms, descending by leaps of forty or fifty feet from one to the other, and forming the most lovely chain of cascades for a length of three or four hundred miles. The walls that shut it in are either perpendicular, or overhanging it in broad table ledges; the wild vegetation of

the forest above, leaning over the chasm with an effect like foliage of a bright translucent green, painted on the sky.

Although but fourteen miles distant from a town containing twelve or fourteen thousand inhabitants, Trenton Falls were unknown till within a very few years. They were discovered by an artist in search of the picturesque, and are now visited, like Niagara and Terni. A quiet but excellent inn, which contrasts strongly, by its respectful service, and its neat and secluded air, with the noisy and carelessly kept hotels of the country, stands on the edge of the pine forest, a little back from the brink of the chasm; and being off the business line of travel, and requiring a little time and expense to reach, it is frequented principally by the better class of travellers, and forms a most agreeable loitering-place, either for the invalid, or the lover of quiet leisure.

In company with the artist to whom the public is indebted for these admirable drawings, I lately visited the ravine by moonlight. We had passed the day in rambling up and down the creek, (a term, by the way, that, differing from its use in England, describes usually in America the finer class of streams;) and I had already made myself familiar by many visits in former years with every turn and phase of its matchless waters, as seen by the light of day. The moon rose about ten, and lifted her perfect orb, without a mist or a cloud, over the shoulder of the mountain which turns the outlet of the ravine. The fine and majestic wood, through which winds the narrow footpath to the Falls, let in the white light in silvery and broken masses—sometimes sliding a long argent line down the dark body of a pine, sometimes pouring in upon the horizontal branches of the hemlock, like an open hand sprinkled with snow; and here and there lighting up a broad circle upon the carpet of tassels and dead leaves, which, in contrast with the heavy shadows of the surrounding wood, looked illuminated with the special brightness of a fairy ring.

We descended the long ladder leading into the ravine, and were soon below the reach of the moonlight, which came slant as yet, and only rimmed the black wall above us with a long strip of white, which, where the wavy line of moss and creepers ran into it, resembled the edging of lace upon a velvet coat in a dark old Flemish picture. The water in this part of the gulf quite fills up the chasm, and rolls, even by day-light, in a black and sullen stream between the bare cliffs which frown over it. The only path here is a giddy ledge, half way up the precipice, which is passed with the aid of a chain run along the rock; and, as we stood on this, looking over into the uncertain darkness below, with the murmur of the far-down and invisible current ascending faintly to our ears, and the light of heaven ceasing so far above us, it seemed to us not an inapt image of the infernal river. We crept on till we came to the foot of the principal Fall, and sat down on the platform below, to wait the gradual descent of the moon.

The mist over the Fall began to show like a film of gauze waving in the air; the sharp angles and crevices in the precipice caught the light one by one, and soon the whole upper ravine was illuminated, while through the gorge below the stream still made its way darkly and solemnly to the outlet.

No pencil, no language, can describe the splendour with which the moon drew her light across the face of the Fall. The other objects in the ravine drank her beams soberly, and gave back only their own calm outlines to the eye; but, from this wall of waters, every spray-drop gave back a diamond—every column of the descending element, a pillar of silver. If there were gates to fairy-land opening from this world of ours, and times when they are visible and recognizable by the chance passing eye of man, I should have believed that we had fallen on the hour, and that some inner and slowly opening portal was letting the brightness of a fairy world through these curtains of crystal.

VIEW FROM MOUNT HOLYOKE.

Probably the richest view in America, in point of cultivation and fertile beauty, is that from Mount Holyoke. The bald face of this mountain, which is turned towards Northampton, is about one thousand one hundred feet above the level of the Connecticut river, (or Quonnecticut, as pronounced by the Indians,) and commands a radius of about sixty miles. The ascent at the side is easy; and it is a fashionable climb for tourists, whose patronage of ginger-beer and sunrises maintains a shanty and a hermit on the top, and keeps in repair a series of scrambling but convenient ladders at the difficult points of the enterprise. The view immediately below presents a singular phase of the scenery of the river, which seems here to possess a soul for beauty, and loiters, enamoured and unwilling to flow on, in the bosom of a meadow which has no parallel in New England for loveliness and fertility. Four times the amorous stream turns to the west, and thrice to the east, threading its silver tide through the tender verdure as capriciously as a vein in the neck of beauty, and cheating twelve miles of direct course into twenty-four of coil and current. The meadow is almost entirely unfenced, and the river is fringed in all its windings with weeping elms, wild flowers and shrubs, while up toward the town the fields rise in slightly swelling terraces—forming a foreground to one of the most sunny and cheerful villages in Massachusetts.

The more extended view embraces a great variety of mountain range—Monadhoe in the north-east, Saddle Mountain in the north-west, Mount Tom (between which and Mount Holyoke the Connecticut seems to have broken with the outlet waters of an immense lake) close on the south-west, and spurs of the Green Mountains advancing and receding in the course of the Connecticut in the north. Geologists speculate extensively on the lakes that once existed in the bosoms formed by these mountains—but we have not time to go back to the deluge.

There is a small hamlet at the foot of Mount Holyoke, on the eastern side of the river, called by the Indian name Hoccanum, and another at the foot of Mount Tom, on the western side, called Pascommuc, both of which were burnt by the savages in the early settlement of the country, and the inhabitants killed or taken captive. The early history of all these towns on the Connecticut river is filled with events of Indian warfare. Northampton, by its rich alluvial land allured the first settlers of Massachusetts long before most of the country between it and the sea-coast possessed an inhabitant. These adventurous pilgrims seated themselves in the midst of an unprotected wilderness, and surrounded by populous Indian tribes; and, first purchasing the land at the Indians' valuation, they defended themselves afterwards as they might from the aggressions of these and others. The township of Northampton (called Nonotuc by the aborigines) was first bought in 1653. It was conveyed to John Pyncheon for the planters by Wawdillowa, Nenessahalant, Nassicochee, and four others (one of whom was a married woman), who were styled the "chief and proper owners." The price was "one hundred fathom of wampum by tale, and ten coats," to which was added an agreement to plough for the Indians, in the ensuing summer, sixteen acres of land on the east side of Quonnecticut River. These "all bargained for themselves, or the other owners by their consent." All the aborigines of this country, observes a correct writer on this subject, are owners of the lands on which they dwell—men and women alike. This property in lands, held by the Indian women, is a singular fact in the history of the savage nations.

Three years after, a rich interval near Northampton, called Capawanke, and containing eight or nine hundred acres, was sold to these same planters by an Indian, named Lampancho, for fifty shillings, at two payments, "to his entire satisfaction."

These two purchases give a very fair idea of the Indian purchases made by our forefathers. In the former, ninety square miles were sold for a hundred fathom of wampum and ten coats! Within this tract were near five thousand acres of interval land, worth at the present time perhaps eight or nine hundred thousand dollars. Unjust as the transaction seems, however, the price was ample to the Indian, who could not have got so much by keeping it, and for whom there was no other purchaser.

The settlers of Nonotuc lived in comparative harmony with the tribe about them; but in the subsequent Indian wars they lived in perpetual fear and agitation. The town was surrounded with palisades, "the meeting-house" was fortified, as were most of the private houses, and several forts were built within the town. Still their dwellings were often burnt, their women and children carried into captivity, and their time was divided between war and agriculture.

OUTLET OF NIAGARA RIVER.

This view is taken from the American side, and presents the debouchure of the waters of Niagara into Lake Ontario, from a point of great advantage. The vastness of the lake beyond, the tremendous agony which the still foaming waters have just escaped at Niagara, and the remoter journey of three thousand miles by which they have sought the sea from their fountains in the west, form a back-ground of imagination to this view, which, realised on the spot, give it a very thrilling interest. It is in itself, however, a landscape of unusually bold character; and the lofty and curving banks of the river are in keeping with its powerful flow, and the immense volume it pours into the lake.

Fort Niagara, on the opposite side, was erected by the French so late as 1751, and was looked upon by them as the key to all these inland seas. They had possession of it about eight years. In the beginning of July, 1759, General Prideaux, with his troops, reinforced by the Indian auxiliaries under Sir William Johnson, advanced to Niagara without the least hinderance—the enemy here not being in sufficient force to throw any impediments in the way. About the middle of July he commenced the siege, which he carried on with great vigour till the twentieth, when he was killed in the trenches. Sir William Johnson, who succeeded him, pressed the siege with great vigour. The enemy, alarmed with the apprehension of losing a place of such importance, resolved to make a last effort for its relief. For this purpose, they assembled about twelve hundred men, drawn from Venango, Presque Isle, and Detroit; and these, with some Indian auxiliaries, were detached, under the command of M. d'Aubry, on an attempt to reinforce the garrison. Sir William Johnson having received intelligence of their design, made a disposition to intercept them in their march. He accordingly detached a considerable body of troops for this service, who, falling in with the enemy very near the lines of the besiegers, a battle was fought, which resulted in the entire defeat of the French, with the capture of their commander, and most of his officers. This battle happened the twenty-fourth of July, and was fought in sight of the French garrison at Niagara. Sir William Johnson immediately after sent Major Harvey to the commandant of the fort, with an order, exhorting him to surrender, which being complied with, the garrison, consisting of about six hundred men, surrendered prisoners of war."

The following letter from Sir William Johnson, reporting his victory, is preserved in the Historical Journal kept by Captain Knox, and printed at the time:—

"I have the honour to acquaint you, by Lieutenant Moncrief, that Niagara surrendered to his Majesty's arms, on the twenty-fifth instant. A detachment of twelve hundred men, with a number of Indians, under the command of Messieurs Aubry and Signery, collected from Detroit, Venango, and Presqu'Isle, made an attempt to reinforce the garrison, the twenty-fourth in the morning; but as I had intelligence of them, I made a disposition to intercept them. The evening before, I ordered the light infantry and piquets to take post on the road upon our left, leading from Niagara Falls to the fort; in the morning, I reinforced these with two companies of grenadiers, and part of the forty-sixth regiment. The action began about half an hour after nine; but they were so well received by the troops in front, and the Indians on their flank, that, in an hour's time, the whole was completely ruined, and all their officers made prisoners, among whom are M. d'Aubry, de Signery, Marin, Repentini, to the number of seventeen. I cannot ascertain the number killed, they are so dispersed among the woods; but their loss is great. As this happened under the eyes of the garrison, I thought proper to send my last summons to the commanding officer, for his surrendering, which he listened to. I inclose you the capitulation: M. Moncrief will inform you of the state of our ammunition and provisions; I hope care will be taken to forward an immediate supply of both to Oswego. As the troops that were defeated yesterday were drawn from those posts which lie in General Stanwig's route, I am in hopes it will be of the utmost consequence to the success of his expedition. The public stores of the garrison, that can be saved from the Indians, I shall order the Assistant Quarter-Master General, and the Clerk of the stores, to take an account of, as soon as possible. As all my attention at present is taken up with the Indians, that the capitulation I have agreed to may be observed, your Excellency will excuse my not being more particular. Permit me to assure you, in the whole progress of the siege, which was severe and painful, the officers and men behaved with the utmost cheerfulness and bravery. I have only to regret the loss of General Prideaux and Colonel Johnson; I endeavoured to pursue the late General's vigorous measures, the good effects of which he deserved to enjoy."

THE PALISADES—HUDSON RIVER.

The first feature of the celebrated banks of the Hudson, which arrests the eye of the traveller after leaving New York, is this singular wall of rock, extending as far onward as he can see, and forming a bold barricade against the river on the side of New Jersey. This singular precipice varies in height from fifty to two hundred feet, and presents a naked front of columnar strata, which gives it its descriptive name. The small sloops which lie along under the shore, loading with building stone from its base, and an occasional shed, diminished to the size of a dog-kennel, across the breadth of the river, are the only marks of life and habitation it presents to the traveller's eye.

With most persons, to mention the Palisades is to recall only the confusion of a steamer's deck, just off from the wharf, with a freight of seven or eight hundred souls hoping to "take tea" in Albany. The scene is one of inextricable confusion, and it is not till the twenty miles of the Palisades are well passed, that the bewildered passenger knows rightly whether his wife, child, or baggage, whichever may be his tender care, is not being left behind at the rate of fifteen miles in the hour.

I have often, when travelling alone, (for "reflection with folded arms" consorts only with the childless and baggageless bachelor), I have often flung my valise into a corner, and sure that the whole of my person and personal effects was under way, watched the maniform embarrassments and troubles that beset the uninitiated voyager on the Hudson. Fifteen minutes before the starting of the boat, there is not a passenger on board; "time is moving," and the American counting it as part of the expense, determines to pay only "on demand." He arrives on the narrow pier at the same instant with seven hundred men, ladies, and children, besides lapdogs, crammed baskets, uncut novels, and baggage for the whole. No commissioner in the world would guarantee to get all this freight on board in the given time, and yet it is done, to the daily astonishment of newspaper hawkers, orange-women, and penny-a-liners watching for dreadful accidents. The plank is drawn in, the wheels begin to paw like foaming steeds impatient to be off, the bell rings as if it was letting down the steps of the last hackney-coach, and away darts the boat, like half a town suddenly slipping off and taking a walk on the water. The "hands," (who follow their nomenclature literally, and have neither eyes nor bowels) trip up all the little children and astonished maids, in coiling up the hawser; the black head-waiter rings a hand-bell as if he were crazy, exhorting "them passengers as hasn't settled to step to the Cap'n's office, and settle," and angry people who have lost sight of their portmanteaus, and selfish people who will not get up to let the young gentleman see if his penny trumpet is not under them, play in a real-life farce better than Keeley or Liston. A painted notice and a very fat black woman in the door-way, inform the gentleman who has not seen his wife since the boat started, and is not at all sure that she is on board, that "no gentleman is permitted to enter the ladies' cabin," and spite of his dreadful uncertainty, he is obliged to trust to this dark Hebe to find her, among three hundred ladies, by description, and amuses all the listeners with his inventory of her dress, features, and general appearance. The negress disappears, is called twenty ways in twenty seconds, and an hour after, the patient husband sees the faithless messenger pass with a glass of lemonade, having utterly forgotten him and the lady in the black bonnet and grey eyes, who may be, for ought he knows to the contrary, wringing her hands at that moment on the wharf at New York. By this time, the young ladies are tired of looking at the Palisades, and have taken out their novels, the old gentlemen are poring over their damp newspapers, and the captain has received his fourteen hundred or two thousand dollars, locked up his office, and gone up to smoke with the black funnel and the engineer. The broad waters of the Tappan Sea open before the flying cut-water; those who have never been up the river before, think of poor André as they pass Tappan and Parrytown, and those who love gentle worth and true genius begin to look out for Sleepy Hollow, and the house of Washington Irving. It is a quiet little spot, buried in trees, and marked with an old Dutch vane. May his latter days, when they shall come, find there the reverence and repose which are his due!

THE RAPIDS ABOVE THE FALLS OF NIAGARA.

During the last Canadian war, General Putnam, the famous partisan soldier, made the first descent upon Goat Island. A wager had been laid, that no man in the army would dare to cross the Rapids from the American side; and with the personal daring for which he was remarkable, above all the men of that trying period, he undertook the feat. Selecting the four stoutest and most resolute men in his corps, he embarked in a batteau just above the island, and with a rope attached to the ring-bolt, which was held by as many muscular fellows on the shore, he succeeded by desperate rowing in reaching his mark. He most easily towed back, and the feat has since been rendered unnecessary by the construction of the bridge from which the accompanying view is taken.

Many years since, a Tonemanta chief, after a violent quarrel with his squaw, lay down to sleep in his canoe. The little bark was moored just out of the tide of Niagara river, at the inlet to the creek which takes its name from his tribe, and the half-drunken chief, with his bottle of rum in his bosom, was soon fast asleep among the sedges. The enraged squaw, finding, after several attempts, that she could not get possession of the bottle without waking him, unmoored the canoe, and swimming out of the creek, pushed it before her into the swift tide of the river. She then turned its head toward the Falls and regained the shore. The canoe floated down very tranquilly till it struck the first ridge of the rapids. Nearly upset by the shock, she was flung from side to side by the contending waters, and the chief started from his slumbers. The first glance convinced him that effort would be vain; and keeping the canoe upright with instinctive skill, he drew his bottle from his bosom, and put it to his lips. The draught lasted him till he reached the turn of the cataract; and, as the canoe shot over the glassy curve, he was seen sitting upright, with his head thrown back, and both hands pressed to the bottle.

Not long ago it was advertised that, on a certain day, a large vessel, freighted with two or three menageries of wild beasts, and some domestic animals, would be sent down the Rapids. The announcement drew together an immense concourse of people from every part of the country, and, at the time specified, the vessel was towed into the stream and abandoned, with the animals loose on her deck. She kept her way very gallantly till she got to the Rapids, when, after a tremendous pitching for a few minutes, she stuck fast in the cleft of a rock. The bears and monkeys were seen in the rigging, but the other animals, not being climbers, were invisible from the shore. To the great disappointment of many thousands, she went over the Falls in the night, and of her whole crew the sole survivor was a goose, who was picked up the next day with no damage but a broken wing, and has since been exhibited as a curiosity.

The Rapids are far from being the least interesting feature of Niagara. There is a violence and a power in their foaming career, which is seen in no other phenomenon of the same class. Standing on the bridge which connects Goat Island with the Main, and looking up towards Lake Erie, the leaping crests of the rapids form the horizon, and it seems like a battle-charge of tempestuous waves, animated and infuriated, against the sky. No one who has not seen this spectacle of turbulent grandeur can conceive with what force the swift and overwhelming waters are flung upwards. The rocks, whose soaring points show above the surface, seem tormented with some supernatural agony, and fling off the wild and hurried waters, as if with the force of a giant's arm. Nearer the plunge of the Fall, the Rapids become still more agitated; and it is almost impossible for the spectator to rid himself of the idea, that they are conscious of the abyss to which they are hurrying, and struggle back in the very extremity of horror. This propensity to invest Niagara with a soul and human feelings is a common effect upon the minds of visitors, in every part of its wonderful phenomena. The torture of the Rapids, the clinging curves with which they embrace the small rocky islands that live amid the surge, the sudden calmness at the brow of the cataract, and the infernal writhe and whiteness with which they reappear, powerless from the depths of the abyss, all seem, to the excited imagination of the gazer, like the natural effects of impending ruin, desperate resolution, and fearful agony, on the minds and frames of mortals.

SARATOGA LAKE.

A singular feature of American scenery is the great number and beauty of its small fresh-water lakes, from one mile to twenty in circumference, fed universally by subjacent and living springs, with outlet rivers which carry off all that is superfluous, and with shores always richly fringed with foliage, and oftenest hilly and picturesque. They lie in the midst of the wild forests, like silver mirrors, tranquil and lovely, mingling a refinement and an elegance with the bold character of the scenery, which contrasts, like Una, with the couchant Lion. Most of them are feeders to the great lakes and rivers. There are counted fifteen which send their waters into Lake Ontario, from the side of New York alone,—a fact which gives a fair idea of their numbers, while it shows the resources, so difficult to conceive, of those vast plains of water.

Saratoga Lake must depend for celebrity on the campaigns of General Burgoyne, and its fish dinners. Of the first, the history has been written and read. Of the last, the

11

traditions are oral; but while appetite returns, and trout venture to the angler's hook, the memory will be renewed. The Springs are distant only three miles; and hither drive the more luxurious visitors of Saratoga, to dine in parties,—those coming early who prefer sympathy with the catastrophe of the fish, and broiling themselves, during the morning, in a flat-bottomed boat among the trout-catchers.

There was a gay party on this lake some six or eight years since, fishing and airing their wit, under the auspices of a belle of some fame and authority. The boat had been pulled into water of five or six feet depth, on the eastern side, and the ladies sat at the ends of their rods, about forty yards from the shore, watching their floats, which lay on the surface of the glassy water like sleeping flies, but, as the old fisherman in the bow could have told them, laughing loud enough to fright even the eels from their appetites. After several hours' bobbing, without bite or nibble, the belle above mentioned discovered that her hook was caught at the bottom. She rose in the stern, to draw it up more easily, and, all the party leaning over at the same time, she lost her balance, and, in falling overboard, upset the boat. For the first minute it was a scene of some terror. The gentlemen were very near drowning the ladies, and the ladies the gentlemen; but the old fisherman, a tall fellow who knew the ground, and was just within his depth, quietly walked about, picking them up one by one, and giving them a hold of the inverted gunwale, and so pushed them safely to shore, suspended round the boat, like herrings on a hoop. Nobody caught cold; other people had caught fish; they dined merrily, and the principal actor in the scene has since been known by the sobriquet of the diving belle.

There is an Indian superstition attached to this lake, which probably had its source in its remarkable loneliness and tranquillity. The Mohawks believed that its stillness was sacred to the Great Spirit, and that, if a human voice uttered a sound upon its waters, the canoe of the offender would instantly sink. A story is told of an Englishwoman, in the early days of the first settlers, who had occasion to cross this lake with a party of Indians, who, before embarking, warned her most impressively of the spell. It was a silent, breathless day, and the canoe shot over the smooth surface of the lake like a shadow. About a mile from the shore, near the centre of the lake, the woman, willing to convince the savages of the weakness of their superstition, uttered a loud cry. The countenances of the Indians fell instantly to the deepest gloom. After a moment's pause, however, they redoubled their exertions, and, in frowning silence, drove the light bark like an arrow over the waters. They reached the shore in safety, and drew up the canoe, and the woman rallied the chief on his credulity. "The Great Spirit is merciful," answered the scornful Mohawk; "He knows that a white woman cannot hold her tongue."

Saratoga Lake is eight miles in length, and a little over two miles broad. It is about eight miles west of Hudson River, which receives its outlet waters under the name of Fish Creek. The same stream, before its entrance into the lake, is called by the sesquipedalian title of Kayaderosseras River. With its pretty maiden name it loses its beauty, and flows forth from its union with the lake, in a dull and murky stream, and so drops sluggishly into the Hudson. Ah! many an edifying homily has been read from a blinder text.

THE COLONNADE OF CONGRESS HALL.
(SARATOGA SPRINGS.)

Congress Hall has for many years held the palm of fashion among the rival Hotels of Saratoga. It is an immense wooden caravanserai, with no pretensions to architecture beyond what is seen in the drawing, and built with the sole view of affording the average accommodations of packed herrings to an indefinite number of persons. The roominess and liberal proportions of the Colonnade are one of those lies of architecture common to

12

the hotels of this country. The traveller passes from the magnificent promise of the outside, to a chamber ten feet by four, situated in a remote gallery, visited once a day by the "boots" and chambermaid. His bed, chair, and wash-stand, resemble those articles as seen in penitentiaries; and if he chance to be ill at night, he might die like a Pagan, "without bell or candle." The arrangements of the house are, of necessity, entirely gregarious. A bell rings at half-past seven in the morning, at which every body who intends to breakfast, must get up; another bell at eight, to the call of which, if he prefers hot omelette to cold, he must be punctual. Dinner and tea exact the same promptitude; and the latter, which in other countries is a thing of no circumstance or importance, becomes, where you dine at two, a meal not willingly missed. "Tea" is at six or half past, and consists of cold meats, hot rolls, Indian cakes, all other kinds of cakes, all kinds of berries, pies, sweetmeats, and jellies, coffee and tea. This is not a matter to be slighted after a fast of four hours; and home hurry beaux and belles from their abbreviated drives, with a loss of sentiment and sunset, and with profit to the keepers of stables, who let their horses "by the afternoon."

After tea, the gentlemen who dressed for dinner and "undressed" for their drive, dress once more for the evening, and the spacious Colonnade is thronged with the five hundred guests of the house, who pace to and fro for an hour, or, if it is a ball night, till the black band have made an orchestra of the tables in the dining-room, and struck up "Hail, Columbia!" A hoop, bound with evergreens, and stuck full of candles, hangs in the centre of the hall (ci-devant dining-room); an audience of all the negroes in the establishment sweetens the breath of heaven as it steals in at the windows; and, as the triumphant music returns a second time to the refrain, the lady Patroness enters on the arm of the gentleman who has the most stock in the Bank, followed in couples by all the gentlemen and ladies who intend to dance or play wall-flower. The black musicians "vex their instruments," and keep time with their heads and heels, as if all their extremities had been hired; the beaux who were interrupted in their declarations by the last chassé, (if they wish to go on with it,) lead out their partners to take the air and a cold,—perhaps a heart,—on the Colonnade; and at eleven, champagne goes round for the ladies, and the gentlemen take "summat to drink" at "the bar;" after which the candles burn brighter, and every body is much more agreeable.

Congress Hall is built very near the principal Spring, which lies in the westerly edge of a swamp. It was first discovered by the tracks of the deer, who frequented it so much as to wear paths to it from the surrounding woods. The mineral water is highly medicinal, and is not unpleasant to the taste. It formerly rose in the bed of a small brook, but it is now hid under the floor of an open colonnade, and discharges nearly a gallon a minute. The disengaged gas breaks through in limpid globules, giving to the surface the appearance of an active simmer. Here, before breakfast, creep the few who come to Saratoga for health; and here, before dinner, saunter those who are in need of a walk, or who wish a tonic for the coming meal. A busy varlet, with a capital of a hooked stick and two tin tumblers, drives a thriving trade here, fishing up the sparkling waters at a cent a glass, for all comers. When the gentleman has swallowed his muriate and four carbonates[1] in proper quantity, a smooth serpentine walk leads to the summit of a prettily wooded hill, where he may either grind himself round a circular rail-road in a self-moving chair, or ramble off to the shade, for a little meditation.

[1]
The analysis of a gallon of Congress water is thus stated:—

Muriate of soda	471.600 grains.
Carbonate of lime	178.474 —

Carbonate of soda   16.500   —
Carbonate of magnesia   3.356   —
Carbonate of iron   6.168   —

_____

Total   676.000   —

ALBANY.

Albany is the second city in the State of New York, in population, wealth, and commerce. It stands on the west bank of the Hudson, and about one hundred and forty-five miles from New York by the river, and near the head of sloop navigation. It is built just over the pitch of an extensive plain, lying between the Mohawk and the Hudson, and has very much the look of a city sliding down hill.

The history of Albany is not very definite, touching its first settlement. The probability seems, that, in 1614, the Dutch erected a fort and trading-house on an island just below the city; and also, in nine years after, a fort, which they called Fort Orange, on the present site. It would appear to have been canonically christened, and has been called at different periods Auralia, Beverwyck, and Williamstadt. "All this time," says the historian, "it was known also by the name of 'The Fuyck.'" The Indian appellation in which it rejoiced was Schaunaugh-ta-da, or Once the pine plains.

Albany is the residence of several of the oldest and wealthiest families in the State; but except this, it is a mere centre of transit—the channel through which passes the vast tide of commerce and travel to the north and west. The Erie and Champlain canals here meet the Hudson; and that which is passed up by this long arm from the sea, is handed over to the great lakes by the other two,—as if old Enceladus had been turned into a "worky," and stood with his long arms between salt water and fresh.

The association most people have with Albany, is that of having lost a portmanteau there. The north-river steam-boats land you with from three to seven hundred passengers upon a narrow pier, in the dusk of the evening, where you find from three to seven hundred individuals (more or less), each of whom seems to have no other object in life, than to persuade you, at that particular instant, to go by a certain conveyance, or to stop at a certain hotel. Upon setting your foot on shore, you find yourself among five or six infuriated gentlemen, two or three of whom walk backward before you, and all talking at the pitch which is necessary to drown the deepening hiss of the escape-valve and each other's voices. If you attempt to reason, you have no sooner satisfied the aforesaid six, that your route, your baggage, and your choice of an hotel, are matters in which they cannot be of the slightest assistance to you, than six more take their places, who must be satisfied as well; and so on in the same order. If you resolutely shut your lips, silence is taken for consent; your baggage is seized, and disappears before you have recovered from your amazement; and your only course is to follow the most importunate of your remaining five persecutors to an hotel; advertise in the next morning's paper for your portmanteau; and wait in Albany till it returns from Canada or Lake Erie, or till you are reconciled to its loss.

One of the most amusing scenes in the world, if it were not so distressing, is to see a large family of rather respectable emigrants landed by the steamer in Albany. It is their first step inland; and with all the confidence of those who are accustomed to countries where a man's person and property are outwardly respected, they yield their children and baggage to the persuasive gentlemen who assure them that all is right; and if a passing wonder crosses the mind of the sufferer, that his route should be so immediately comprehended by a perfect stranger, it is chased away the next moment by his surprise at

14

the scene of bustle and confusion. At the end of five minutes the crowd thins a little, and he looks about for his family and effects. A stage coach is dashing off at top-speed in one direction, with his eldest daughter stretching out of the window, and crying in vain that there is some mistake; his two youngest are on board a steam-boat just off from the pier, and bound eight miles further up the river: the respectable part of his baggage has entirely disappeared; and nothing but his decrepit grandmother and the paternal bedstead (both indebted for their escape to being deaf, and not portable,) remain of his family and chattels. For his comfort, the gentry around inform him that his children may be got back in a day or two, and he may find his baggage somewhere on his route to the west— offering, for a consideration not very trifling, to send off an express for either one or the other.

Albany is the seat of government, and has a State House, of which the historian of New York remarks: "In the structure of this edifice, the rules of architecture, whether Egyptian, Hindoo, Chinese, Grecian, Roman, Saracenic, Gothic, or Composite, have been violated." Lately, however, a taste for a better style of architecture seems to prevail; and in North Pearl-street we lately noticed a façade (we think, of a new church,) in a very pure and beautiful style. The private houses of Albany are built, many of them, very expensively; and the city is remarkable for its hospitality.

CROW NEST, FROM BULL HILL, WEST POINT.

It is true of the Hudson, as of all other rivers, that, to be seen to advantage, it should form the middle, not the foreground of the picture. Those who go to Albany by steam have something the same idea of the scenery of West Point, that an inside passenger may have of the effect of the Brighton coach at top-speed. It is astonishing how much foreground goes for in landscape; and there are few passes of scenery where it is more naturally beautiful than those of the Hudson. In the accompanying drawing, the picturesque neighbourhood of Undercliff, the seat of Colonel Morris, lies between the river and the artist, and directly opposite stands the peak of Crow Nest, mentioned in the description of West Point.

Crow Nest is one of the most beautiful mountains of America for shape, verdure, and position; and when the water is unruffled, and the moon sits on his summit, he looks like a monarch crowned with a single pearl. This is the scene of the first piece-work of fancy which has come from the practical brain of America,—the poem of The Culprit Fay. The opening is so descriptive of the spot, that it is quite in place here; and to those who have not seen the poem (as most European readers have not) it will convey an idea of a production which, in my opinion, treads close on the heels of the Midsummer Night's Dream:—

"'Tis the middle watch of a summer's night,—
The earth is dark, but the heavens are bright;
Nought is seen in the vault on high,
But the moon, and the stars, and the cloudless sky,
And the flood which rolls its milky hue,—
A river of light on the welkin blue.
The moon looks down on old Crow Nest,
She mellows the shades on his shaggy breast
And seems his huge grey form to throw
In a silver cone on the wave below;
His sides are broken by spots of shade,
By the walnut boughs and the cedar made,

And through their clustering branches dark
Glimmers and dies the firefly's spark,—
Like starry twinkles that momently break
Through the rifts of the gathering tempest rack.
The stars are on the moving stream,
And fling, as its ripples gently flow,
A burnish'd length of wavy beam,
In an eel-like, spiral line below.
The winds are whist, and the owl is still,
The bat in the shelvy rock is hid;
And nought is heard on the lonely hill
But the cricket's chirp and the answer shrill
    Of the gauze-wing'd raty-did;
And the plaints of the mourning whip-poor-will,
Who mourns unseen, and ceaseless sings
Ever a note of wail and wo,
Till morning spreads her rosy wings,
And earth and skies in her glances glow.
'Tis the hour of fairy ban and spell:
The wood-tick has kept the minutes well;
He has counted them all with click and stroke
Deep in the heart of the mountain-oak;
And he has awakened the sentry-elve,
Who sleeps with him in the haunted tree,
To bid him ring the hour of twelve,
And call the fays to their revelry.

       * * * * * * * * *

They come from beds of lichen green,
They creep from the mullen's velvet screen;
Some on the backs of beetles fly
From the silver tops of moon-touch'd trees,
Where they swing in their cob-web hammocks high,
And rock'd about in the evening breeze;
Some from the hum-bird's downy nest,
They had driven him out by elfin power,
And pillow'd on plumes of his rainbow breast,
Had slumber'd there till the charmed hour;
Some had lain in a scarp of the rock,
With glittering rising-stars inlaid,
And some had open'd the four-o'clock,
And stolen within its purple shade:
And now they throng the moonlight glade,
Above—below—on every side,
Their little minion forms arrayed
In the tricksy pomp of fairy pride.'

The general assembly of the fairies is at last complete, and they proceed to the trial
of the culprit fay, who has extinguished his elfin lamp and paralyzed his wings by a love
for a mortal maid. He is condemned to penances, which are most exquisitely described,

and constitute the greater part of the poem; and he finally expiates his sins, and is forgiven. There is a fineness of description, and a knowledge of the peculiarities of American nature, in birds, fishes, flowers, and the phenomena of this particular region, which constitute this little poem a book of valuable information as well as an exquisite work of fancy.

Just under Crow Nest, buried in the heavy leaves of a ravine, springs a waterfall like a Naiad from the depths of the forest, and plunges down into the river. The rambles in and about its neighbourhood are cool and retired; and it is a favourite place for lovers from New York, who run up in the steamer in three hours, and find the honeymoon goes swimmingly off there,—the excellent hotel within half a mile supplying the real, without which the ideal is found to be very trumpery. The marble tomb of a cadet, who was killed by the bursting of a gun, forms a picturesque object, and gives a story to the spot.

VIEW BELOW TABLE ROCK.

The interest of the view under this impending cliff is somewhat heightened by the probability that it will fall into the abyss sometime within the next six months. Since the fall of the most projecting part of it, two or three winters since, a large and very deep crack has widened around the remaining area of the platform above, and it is thought that it will scarce survive the next frost. At present, spite of the threat, troops of ladies and gentlemen crowd its broad summit at all hours, walking, drawing, gazing, and philandering, in the fullest confidence that rocks have bases. And so it will go on, probably, till the "one (thunder) too many" hammers through its crack of doom.

The path leading behind the sheet of Horse Shoe Fall, runs close under the cliff of Table Rock; and between the spray and the small rivulets that trickle over the sharp edge, or find their way out of the numerous crevices on the face of the precipice, it is as wet as the lawn blessed with "perpetual rain" by the Witch of Atlas. We were of a considerable party that visited this Naiad's palace in the close of the last summer. A small shanty stands at the head of the staircase, kept by a very civil Englishman, who, with the assistance of his daughter and two sons, keeps a reading-room and registry, vends curious walking-sticks cut at Niagara, minerals, spars, and stuffed scorpions, besides officiating as guide under the Falls, and selling brandy and water to those who survive the expedition.

The ladies of the party were taken into a small apartment to change their dresses preparatory to their descent; and the two smart lads of our conductor soon metamorphosed their cavaliers into as brigand-looking a set of tatterdemallions as could be found in the Abruzzi. Rough duck trowsers, long jackets of green painted cloth, oil-skin hats, and flannel shirts,—the whole turn-out very much like the clothes of the drowned exhibited for recognition at the Moague in Paris,—constituted our habiliments. The difference of the female costume consisted in the substitution of a coarse petticoat for the trowsers, and a string tied over the broad-brimmed hat;—and, flattery aside, our friends would have looked at home in Billingsgate. Quite the most formidable part of the expedition, to them, was passing in review before some twenty curious persons collected on the way.

The guide went before, and we followed close under the cliff. A cold clammy wind blew strong in our faces from the moment we left the shelter of the staircase; and a few steps brought us into a pelting, fine rain, that penetrated every opening of our dresses, and made our foothold very slippery and difficult. We were not yet near the sheet of water we were to walk through; but one or two of the party gave out and returned, declaring it was impossible to breathe; and the rest, imitating the guide, bent nearly double to keep the beating spray from their nostrils, and pushed on, with enough to do to keep sight of his heels. We arrived near the difficult point of our progress; and in the midst of a confusion of blinding gusts, half deafened, and more than half drowned, the guide stopped to give us a hold of his skirts and a little counsel. All that could be heard amid the thunder of the cataract beside us was an injunction to push on when it got to the worst, as it was shorter to get beyond the sheet than to go back; and with this pleasant statement of our dilemma, we faced about with the longest breath we could draw, and encountered the enemy. It may be supposed that every person who has been draped through the column of water which obstructs the entrance to the cavern behind this cataract, has a very tolerable idea of the pains of drowning. What is wanting in the density of the element is more than made up by the force of the contending winds, which rush into the mouth, eyes, and nostrils, as if flying from a water-fiend. The "courage of worse behind" alone persuades the gasping sufferer to take one desperate step more.

It is difficult enough to breathe within; but with a little self-control and management, the nostrils may be guarded from the watery particles in the atmosphere, and then an impression is made upon the mind by the extraordinary pavilion above and around, which never loses its vividness. The natural bend of the falling cataract, and the backward shelve of the precipice, form an immense area like the interior of a tent, but so pervaded by discharges of mist and spray, that it is impossible to see far inward. Outward the light struggles brokenly through the crystal wall of the cataract; and when the sun shines directly on its face, it is a scene of unimaginable glory. The footing is rather unsteadfast, a small shelf composed of loose and slippery stones; and the abyss below boils like—it is difficult to find a comparison. On the whole, this undertaking is rather pleasanter to remember than to achieve.

LAKE WINIPISEOGEE,
(THE BEAUTIFUL LAKE OF THE INDIANS,)

NEW HAMPSHIRE.

The Indian fights of the celebrated Captain Lovewell, which took place near the borders of this lake, were not the only feats of courage the early inhabitants of this part of the country were called upon to display. Bears, wolves, and catamounts, were enemies as constantly found in their path as the unfriendly Indian, and were almost as dangerous. The descriptions contained in the grave historical records of the State, of encounters, with bears more particularly, are sometimes sufficiently amusing; and, indeed, whatever the peril to the man, there is a conventional drollery about the bear which throws a spice of fun into all his contests with mankind. This animal, in the early days of New Hampshire, often destroyed the husbandman's hopes by his depredations on the green maize, of the milky ear of which he is especially fond. Sweet fruits, honey, and other simple but "toothsome" productions of the orchard and farm, suited bruin equally well, and he had never recourse to animal food while these were to be procured. The kind of bear most mischievous in this way was the small American bear, with a long and pointed nose, remarkable for his alertness in ascending and descending trees. They were often found in hollow trunks, and in clefts of rocks, and were considered delicious meat by the hunters. Among the adventures with this class of their enemies recorded of the first settlers of the State, is an encounter of a Mr. Annis with a bear.

"One day, late in March," says the narrator, "the snow being deep, he mounted his snow-shoes, and in company with Abner Watkins and their dogs, set off towards the Mink Hills for a hunt, armed with an axe and gun. In the neighbourhood of the hills, the dogs were perceived to be very much excited with something in a ledge of rocks. Annis

18

left his companion, Watkins, and ascended a crag twenty or thirty feet to where the dogs were, having no other weapon with him but his staff, which was pointed with iron. After exploring a little, he concluded there was no game there of more consequence than a hedge-hog or some other small animal, and being fatigued laid down in the snow on his back to rest, reclining his head upon the place he had been examining; he had but just laid down when he heard a snuffling under his ear; he started up, and turning round, found an old bear pressing her head up through the old leaves and snow which filled the mouth of her den; he thrust his spear-pointed staff at the bear's briskets, and thus held the bear which was pressing towards him at his staff's length distance, and called to his companion Watkins to come up with the axe and kill the bear, which, after some little time, was effected. After the action was over, Annis complained of Watkins' dilatoriness, but Watkins excused himself by saying he could not get his gun off, that he had snapt, snapt, snapt several times. Where did you take sight? said Annis, knowing that he was directly between him and the bear; I took sight between your legs, said Watkins."

Many years ago a cub bear was caught by a stout lad near the borders of Lake Winipiseogee, carried into town, and after proper drilling, became the playfellow of the boys of the village, and often accompanied them to the school-house. After passing a few months in civilized society, he made his escape to the woods, and after a few years was almost forgotten. The school-house meantime had fallen from the schoolmaster's to the schoolmistress's hands, and in the room of large boys and girls learning to write and cipher, small boys and girls were taught in the same place knitting and spelling. One winter's day, after a mild fall of snow, the door had been left ajar by some urchin going out, when to the unutterable horror of the spectacled dame and her fourscore hopeful abecedarians, an enormous bear walked in, in the most familiar manner in the world, and took a seat by the fire. Huddling over the benches with what expedition they might, the children crowded about their schoolmistress, who had fled to the farthest corner of the room, and stood crying and pushing to escape the horror of being eaten first. The bear sat snuffing and warming himself by the fire, however, exhibiting great signs of satisfaction, but deferring his meal till he had warmed himself thoroughly. The screams of the children continued, but the school-house was far from any other habitation, and the bear did not seem at all embarrassed by the outcry. After sitting and turning himself about for some time, Bruin got up on his hind legs, and shoving to the door, began to take down, one by one, the hats, bonnets, and satchels, that hung on several rows of pegs behind it. His memory had not deceived him, for they contained, as of old, the children's dinners, and he had arrived before the recess. Having satisfied himself with their cheese, bread, pies, dough-nuts, and apples, Bruin smelt a little at the mistress's desk, but finding it locked, gave himself a shake of resignation, opened the door and disappeared. The alarm was given, and the amiable creature was pursued and killed,—very much to the regret of the townspeople, when it was discovered by some marks on his body that it was their old friend and playfellow.

KOSCIUSKO'S MONUMENT.
A pretty marble shaft stands on the edge of the broad highland esplanade of West Point, overlooking the most beautiful scene on the most beautiful river of our country. It commemorates the virtues of Kosciusko, who, during his second sojourn in America, lived at West Point, and cultivated his little garden, near the site of this tribute to his memory. Kosciusko's first laurels were gained in this country under Washington. He was educated in the military school at Warsaw, whence he was sent, as one of four, to complete his education at Paris. On his return to Poland, he had a commission given him,

19

but, being refused promotion, he determined to come to America, and join the colonies in their struggle for independence. With letters from Dr. Franklin to General Washington, he presented himself to the great patriot, and was immediately appointed his aid-de-camp, and later he received the appointment to the engineers, with the rank of colonel. At the close of the war, having distinguished himself by his courage and skill, he returned to Poland, was appointed major-general in the army of the diet, and served as general of division under the younger Poniatowski. Finding, however, his efforts for freedom paralysed by the weakness or treachery of others, he gave in his resignation, and went into retirement at Leipsic. He was still there in 1793, when the Polish army and people gave signs of being in readiness for insurrection. All eyes were turned towards Kosciusko, who was at once chosen for their leader, and messengers were sent to him from Warsaw to acquaint him with the schemes and wishes of his compatriots. In compliance with the invitation, he proceeded towards the frontiers of Poland; but apprehensive of compromising the safety of those with whom he acted, he was about to defer his enterprise, and set off for Italy. He was fortunately persuaded to return, and, arriving at Cracow at the very time when the Polish garrison had expelled the Russian troops, he was chosen generalissimo, with all the power of a Roman dictator. He immediately published an act, authorizing insurrection against the foreign authorities, and proceeded to support Colonel Madalinski, who was pursued by the Russians. Having joined that officer, they gained their first victory, defeating the enemy with inferior numbers. His army now increased to nine thousand men, the insurrection extended to Warsaw, and in a few days the Russians were driven from that palatinate. He obtained some advantage over the enemy in one more contest, but the king of Prussia arriving to the assistance of the Russians, he was exposed to great personal danger, and suffered a defeat. From this period he waged a disadvantageous warfare against superior force, and at last at Maczienice (or Maniejornice), fifty miles from Warsaw, an overwhelming Russian force completely defeated Kosciusko. He fell from his horse wounded, saying Finis Poloniæ, and was made prisoner.

Kosciusko was sent to Russia, and confined in a fortress near St. Petersburgh, where he was kept till the accession of Paul I. This monarch, through real or affected admiration for the character of the great man, released him, and presented him with his sword: "I have no longer occasion for a sword, since I have no longer a country," answered Kosciusko.

In 1797 he once more took his departure for the United States, where he was received with honour and warm welcome by the grateful people whose liberty he had aided to achieve. He was granted a pension by the government, and elected to the society of the Cincinnati. He returned to Europe the following year, bought an estate near Fontainebleau, and lived there till 1814. He removed again to Switzerland, and established himself at Soleure, where he died, in consequence of a fall with his horse over a precipice near Vevay. Among the last acts of his life, were the emancipation of the slaves on his own estate in Poland, and a bequest for the emancipation and education of slaves in Virginia.

Kosciusko was never married. His body was removed to Cracow, and deposited with great state in the tomb of the kings beneath the cathedral. The oldest officers were his bearers; two beautiful young girls with wreathes of oak leaves and cypress followed, and then came a long procession of the general staff, senate, clergy, and people. Count Wodsiki delivered a funeral oration on the hill of Wavel, and a prelate delivered an eloquent address in the church. The senate decreed that a lofty mound should be erected on the heights of Bronislawad. For three years men of every age and class toiled gratuitously at this work, and at last the Mogila Kosziuszki, the mound of Kosciusko, was raised to the height of 3000 feet! A serpentine path leads to the top, from which there is a noble view of the Vistula, and of the ancient city of the Polish kings. The small monument at West Point has less pretension, but it is the exponent of as deep a debt of gratitude, and of as grateful and universal honour to his memory.

HORSESHOE FALLS, AT NIAGARA.
(SEEN FROM GOAT ISLAND.)

Niagara is the outlet of several bodies of water, covering, it is estimated, 150,000 square miles! Dr. Dwight considers the Falls as part of the St. Lawrence, following that river back to the sources near the Mississippi; and, doing away with the intermediate names of St. Marie, Detroit, St. Clair, Iroquois, and Cataraqui, he traces its course through the lakes Superior, Huron, Erie, and Ontario, as the Rhone is followed through the Lake of Geneva, and the Rhine through Lake Constance. In this view the St. Lawrence is doubtless the first river in the world. It meets the tide of the sea four hundred miles from its mouth, which is ninety-five miles broad; and to this height fleets of men of war may ascend and find ample room for an engagement. Merchantmen of all sizes go up to Montreal, which is six hundred miles from the sea; and its navigation for three thousand miles is only interrupted in three places,—Niagara Falls, the rapids of the Iroquois, and the part called the river St. Marie. The St. Marie is navigable for boats, though not for larger vessels; a portage of ten miles (soon to be superseded by a ship canal) conveys merchandise around the Falls of Niagara, and the rapids of the Iroquois present so slight a hinderance, that goods are brought from Montreal to Queenston for nearly the same price as they would pay by unobstructed navigation.

It is necessary to remember the extent of the waters which feed Niagara, to conceive, when standing for an hour only on the projecting rocks, how this almighty wonder can go on so long. Even then,—that these inland seas lie above, tranquil and unexhausted, scarce varying their high-water mark perceptibly, from year to year, yet supplying, for every hour, the "ninety millions of tons," which, it is estimated, plunge over the cataract,—it affords you a standard for the extent of those lakes, to which the utmost stretch of the mind seems scarcely competent.

The accompanying view from Goat Island is of course only partial, as the American fall is entirely left out of the picture. The Horseshoe Falls, as a single object, however, is unquestionably the sublimest thing in nature. To know that the angle of the cataract, from the British shore to the tower, is near half a mile in length; that it falls so many feet with so many tons of water a minute; or even to see it, as here, admirably represented by the pencil; conveys no idea to the reader of the impression produced on the spectator. One of the most remarkable things about Niagara is entirely lost in the drawing—its motion. The visitor to Niagara should devote one day exclusively to the observation of this astonishing feature. The broad flood glides out of Lake Erie with a confiding tranquillity that seems to you, when you know its impending destiny, like that of a human creature advancing irresistibly, but unconsciously, to his death. He embraces the bright islands that part his arms for a caress; takes into his bosom the calm tribute of the Tonewanta and Unnekuqua—small streams that come drowsing through the wilderness—and flows on, till he has left Lake Erie far behind, bathing the curving sides of his green shores with a surface which only the summer wind ruffles. The channel begins to descend; the still unsuspecting waters fall back into curling eddies along the banks, but the current in the centre flows smoothly still. Suddenly the powerful stream is flung with accumulated swiftness among broken rocks; and, as you watch it from below, it seems tossed with the first shock into the very sky. It descends in foam, and from this moment its agony commences. For three miles it tosses and resists, and, racked at every step by sharper rocks and increased rapidity, its unwilling and choked waves fly back, to be again precipitated onward, and at last reach the glossy curve, convulsed with supernatural horror. They touch the emerald arch, and in that instant, like the calm that follows the conviction of inevitable doom, the agitation ceases,—the waters pause,—the foam and resistance subside into a transparent stillness,—and slowly and solemnly the vexed and tormented sufferer drops into the abyss. Every spectator, every child, is struck with the singular deliberation, the unnatural slowness, with which the waters of Niagara take their plunge. The laws of gravitation seem suspended, and the sublimity of the tremendous gulf below seems to check the descending victim on the verge, as if it paused in awe.

THE NARROWS, AT STATEN ISLAND.

Almost any land looks beautiful after a long voyage; and it would not be surprising if the Narrows, oftenest seen and described by those who have just come off the passage of the Atlantic, should have this reputation. It does not require an eye long deprived of verdure, however, to relish the bold shores, the bright green banks, the clustering woods, and tasteful villas, which make up the charms of this lovely strait.

Busier waters than the Narrows could scarcely be found; and it is difficult to imagine, amid so much bustle and civilisation, the scene that presented itself to Hendrick Hudson, when the little Halve-Mane stole in on her voyage of discovery two hundred years ago. Hoofden, or the Highlands, as he then named the hills in this neighbourhood, "were covered with grass and wild-flowers, and the air was filled with fragrance." Groups of friendly natives, clothed in elk skins, stood on the beach, singing, and offering him welcome, and, anchoring his little bark, he explored with his boats the channel and inlets, and penetrated to the mouth of the river which was destined to bear his name. It appears, however, that the Indians on the Long Island side were less friendly; and in one of the excursions into the Bay of Manhattan, his boat was attacked by a party of twenty-nine savages of a ferocious tribe, and an English sailor, named Colman, was killed by an arrow-shot in the shoulder. Other unfriendly demonstrations from the same tribe, induced Hudson to leave his anchorage at Sandy Hook, and he drew in to the Bay of New York, which he found most safe and commodious, and where he still continued his intercourse with the Indians of Staten Island, receiving them on board his vessel, dressing them, to their extravagant delight, in red coats, and purchasing from them fish and fruits in abundance.

At this day there stands a villa on every picturesque point; a thriving town lies on the left shore; hospitals and private sanitary establishments extend their white edifices in the neighbourhood of the quarantine-ground; and between the little fleets of merchantmen, lying with the yellow flag at their peak, fly rapidly and skilfully a constant succession of steam-boats, gaily painted and beautifully modelled, bearing on their airy decks the population of one of the first cities of the world. Yet of Manhattan Island, on which New York is built, Hudson writes, only two hundred years ago, that "it was wild and rough; a thick forest covered the parts where anything would grow; its beach was broken and sandy, and full of inlets; its interior presented hills of stony and sandy alluvion, masses of rock, ponds, swamps, and marshes."

The gay description which an American would probably give of the Narrows,—the first spot of his native land seen after a tedious voyage,—would probably be in strong contrast with the impression it produces on the emigrant, who sees in it only the scene of his first difficult step in a land of exile. I remember noting this contrast with some

22

emotion, on board the packet-ship in which I was not long ago a passenger from England. Among the crowd of emigrants in the steerage, was the family of a respectable and well-educated man, who had failed as a merchant in some small town in England, and was coming, with the wreck of his fortune, to try the back-woods of America. He had a wife, and eight or ten very fine children, the eldest of whom, a delicate and pretty girl of eighteen, had contributed to sustain the family under their misfortunes at home, by keeping a village school. The confinement had been too much for her, and she was struck with consumption—a disease which is peculiarly fatal in America. Soon after leaving the British Channel, the physician on board reported her to the captain as exceedingly ill, and suffering painfully from the close air of the steerage; and by the general consent of the cabin passengers, a bed was made up for her in the deck-house, where she received the kindest attention from the ladies on board; and with her gentle manners and grateful expressions of pleasure, soon made an interest in all hearts. As we made the land, the air became very close and hot; and our patient, perhaps from sympathy with the general excitement about her, grew feverish and worse, hourly. Her father, and a younger sister, sat by her, holding her hands and fanning her; and when we entered the Narrows with a fair wind, and every one on board, forgetting her in their admiration of the lovely scene, mounted to the upper deck, she was raised to the window, and stood with the bright red spot deepening on her cheek, watching the fresh green land without the slightest expression of pleasure. We dropped anchor, the boats were lowered, and as the steerage passengers were submitted to a quarantine, we attempted to take leave of her before going on shore. A fit of the most passionate tears, the paroxysms of which seemed almost to suffocate her, prevented her replying to us; and we left that poor girl surrounded with her weeping family, trying in vain to comfort her. Hers were feelings, probably, which are often associated with a remembrance of the Narrows.

VIEW OF THE CAPITOL AT WASHINGTON.

There are many favourable points of view for this fine structure, standing, as it does, higher than the general level of the country. Besides those presented in the different drawings in this work, there are views from the distant eminences, which are particularly fine, in which the broad bosom of the Potomac forms the back-ground. The effect of the building is also remarkably imposing when the snow is on the ground, and the whole structure, rising from a field of snow, with its dazzling whiteness, looks like some admirable creation of the frost. All architecture, however, is very much improved by the presence of a multitude of people, and the Capitol looks its best on the day of inauguration. The following description, written after viewing the ceremony of Mr. Van Buren's induction into office, will give an idea of the effect of this solemnity on the architecture:—

"The sun shone out of heaven without a cloud on the inaugural morning. The air was cold, but clear and life-giving, and the broad avenues of Washington for once seemed not too large for the thronging population. The crowds who had been pouring in from every direction for several days before, ransacking the town for but a shelter from the night, were apparent on the spacious side walks, and the old campaigners of the winter seemed but a thin sprinkling among the thousands of new and strange faces. The sun shone alike on the friends and opponents of the new administration; and, as far as one might observe in a walk to the Capitol, all were made cheerful alike by its brightness. It was another augury, perhaps, and may foretell a more extended fusion under the light of the luminary new-risen. In a whole day, passed in a crowd composed of all classes and parties, I heard no remark that the president would have been unwilling to hear.

"I was at the Capitol a half-hour before the procession arrived, and had leisure to study a scene for which I was not at all prepared. The noble staircase of the east front of the building leaps over three arches; under one of which carriages pass to the basement door; and, as you approach from the gate, the eye cuts the ascent at right angles, and the sky, broken by a small spire at a short distance, is visible beneath. Broad stairs occur at equal distances, with corresponding projections, and from the upper platform rise the outer columns of the portico, with ranges of columns three deep extending back to the pilasters. I had often admired this front, with its many graceful columns and its superb flight of stairs, as one of the finest things I had seen in the world. Like the effect of the assembled population of Rome waiting to receive the blessing before the front of St. Peter's, however, the assembled crowd on the steps and at the base of the Capitol, heightened inconceivably the grandeur of the design. They were piled up like the people on the temples of Babylon in one of Martin's sublime pictures—every projection covered, and an inexpressible soul and character given by their presence to the architecture. Boys climbed about the bases of the columns, single figures stood on the posts of the surrounding railings in the boldest relief against the sky, and the whole thing was exactly what Paul Veronese would have delighted to draw.

"I was in the crowd thronging the opposite side of the court, and lost sight of the principal actors in this imposing drama till they returned from the Senate Chamber. A temporary platform had been laid and railed in on the broad stair which supports the portico, and, for all preparation for one of the most important and most meaning and solemn ceremonies on earth—for the inauguration of a chief magistrate over a republic of fifteen millions of freemen—the whole addition to the open air and the presence of the people, was a volume of Holy Writ. In comparing the impressive simplicity of this consummation of the wishes of a mighty people, with the ceremonial and hollow show which embarrass a corresponding event in other lands, it was impossible not to feel that the moral sublime was here—that a transaction so important, and of such extended and weighty import, could borrow nothing from drapery or decoration, and that the simple presence of the sacred volume, consecrating the act, spoke more thrillingly to the heart than the trumpets of a thousand heralds.

"The crowd of diplomatists and senators in the rear of the columns made way, and the ex-President and Mr. Van Buren advanced with uncovered heads. A murmur of feeling rose up from the moving mass below, and the infirm old man, emerged from a sick chamber which his physician had thought it impossible he should leave, bowed to the people, and, still uncovered in the cold air, took his seat beneath the portico. Mr. Van Buren then advanced, and with a voice remarkably distinct, and with great dignity, read his address to the people.

"When the address was closed, the Chief Justice advanced and administered the oath. As the book touched the lips of the new President, there arose a general shout, an expression of feeling common enough in other countries, but drawn with difficulty from an American assemblage. The sons and immediate friends of Mr. Van Buren then closed around him, the ex-President and others gave him the hand in congratulation, and the ceremony was over."

VIEW OF THE RUINS OF FORT TICONDEROGA.

Three weeks before the first battle of the revolution at Lexington, an emissary was sent to Canada by the Committee of Correspondence in Boston, to ascertain the feelings of the people, and to make such reports as his observations might suggest. His first advice was that Ticonderoga should be seized as quickly as possible.

The "Green Mountain Boys" were at this time fresh from their resistance to the new grants, and were immediately fixed upon as the best force to achieve this object. The little army, already organized under the famous Ethan Allen, assembled at Castleton, and the main body, consisting of one hundred and forty men, marched directly to the shore of the lake, opposite Ticonderoga. It was important to have a guide who was acquainted with the ground around the fortress and the places of access. Allen made inquiries as to these points of Mr. Beman, a farmer residing near the lake, who answered that he seldom crossed the Ticonderoga, and was little acquainted with the particulars of its situation; but that his son, Nathan, a young lad, passed much of his time there in company with the boys of the garrison.

The boy was called, and appeared by his answers to be familiar with every nook in the fort, and every passage and by-path by which it could be approached. In the eye of Allen, he was the very person to thread out the best avenue; and by the consent of the father, and a little persuasion, he was engaged to be the guide of the party.

The next step was to procure boats, which were very deficient in number. Eighty-three men only had crossed when the day began to dawn; and while the boats were sent back for the rear division, Allen resolved to move immediately against the fort.

He drew up his men in three ranks, addressed them in a short harangue, and, placing himself at the head of the centre file, led them silently, but with a quick step, up the heights of the fortress. Before the sun rose, he had entered the gate, and formed his men on the parade between the barracks. As Allen passed the gate, a sentinel snapped his fusee at him, and then retreated under a covered way. Another sentinel made a thrust at an officer with his bayonet, and slightly wounded him, but Allen cut him over the head with his sword, and he threw down his musket and asked for quarter. Standing on the parade-ground they gave three huzzas and aroused the sleepers. Allen inquired the way to the commandant's apartment, hastily ascended the stairs, and called out with his stentorian voice at the door, ordering the astonished captain instantly to appear. Startled at so strange and unexpected a summons, he sprang from his bed and opened the door, when the first salutation of his boisterous and unseasonable visitor was an order immediately to surrender the fort. Rubbing his eyes, and trying to collect his scattered senses, the Frenchman asked by what authority he presumed to make such a demand. "In the name of the Great Jehovah and the Continental Congress!" replied Allen.

Not accustomed to hear much of the Continental Congress in this remote corner, nor to respect its authority when he did, the commandant began to speak; but Allen cut shore the thread of his discourse by lifting his sword over his head, and reiterating the demand for an instant surrender. Having neither permission to argue, nor power to resist, Captain De la Place submitted, ordering his men to parade without arms, and the garrison was given up to the victors.

This surprise was effected about four o'clock in the morning on the 10th of May. The remainder of the troops arrived after the fort was taken, and the prisoners, consisting of a captain, a lieutenant, and forty-eight subalterns and privates, were sent on to Hartford under an escort.

As soon as the bustle was over, Allen sent off a detachment to take Crown Point, a small fortress higher up the lake. Strong head winds drove back the boats, and the party returned the same evening. The attempt was renewed a day or two afterwards, and the garrison, consisting of a serjeant and eleven men, were brought in prisoners.

The principal advantage of these captures, besides the possession of the posts, was the acquisition, at Ticonderoga, of one hundred and twenty pieces of cannon, some swivels, mortars, and small arms; and at Crown Point, of sixty-one cannon and some small stores.

The Green Mountain Boys were at this time under sentence of outlawry from the Provincial Government; but after the good service they had done at Ticonderoga, they were formed into a separate regiment, and permitted to nominate their own officers. Their services to the cause of Independence are well known.

VIEW FROM FORT PUTNAM.

This fort, which commands the military position of West Point, and which was considered so important during the revolutionary war, is now in ruins, and is visited by all travellers for the superb view which it affords of the sublime pass of the Highlands. This was the great key which Arnold's treachery intended to give into the hands of the English; and, associated with the memory of the unfortunate André, and with other painful events of the conspiracy, it possesses an interest which is wanting to other objects of the same description in our country.

Washington's visit of inspection to Fort Putnam, and the other redoubts on this side the river, was made only two or three hours before his discovery of the treason of Arnold, at that moment as he supposed in command at West Point. The commander-in-chief was expected to arrive the evening before, and had he done so, Arnold would probably never have escaped. Having accidentally met the French minister, M. de Lucerne, at Fishkill, however (eight miles above), he was induced to pass the night there for the purpose of some conference, and set off early in the morning on horseback, sending on a messenger to Mrs. Arnold that himself and suite would be with her to breakfast. Arriving opposite West Point, near a small redoubt called Fort Constitution, Washington turned his horse from the road. Lafayette, who was then in his suite, called out, "General, you are going in the wrong direction; you know Mrs. Arnold is waiting breakfast for us." "Ah," answered Washington, "I know you young men are all in love with Mrs. Arnold, and wish to get where she is as soon as possible. Go and take your breakfast with her, and tell her not to wait for me: I must ride down and examine the redoubts on this side the river." Two of the aides rode on, found breakfast waiting, and sat down at once with General Arnold and his family. While they were at table, a messenger came in with a letter for Arnold, which announced the capture of André, and the failure and betrayal, of course, of the whole conspiracy. Showing little or no emotion, though his life hung upon a thread, he merely said to one of his aides that his presence was required at West Point; and, leaving word for General Washington that he was called over the river, but would return immediately, he ordered a horse and sent for Mrs. Arnold to her chamber. He then informed her abruptly that they must part, possibly for ever, and that his life depended on his reaching the enemy's lines without delay. Struck with horror at this intelligence, she swooned and fell senseless. In that state he left her, hurried down stairs, mounted a horse belonging to one of his aides that stood saddled at the door, and rode with all speed to the bank of the river. A boat with six men was in waiting; and, pretending that he was going with a flag of truce, he pulled down the stream, and arrived safe on board the Vulture sloop of war, lying some miles below.

Having finished his inspection of the redoubt, Washington arrived at Arnold's house, received the message, and concluded to cross immediately and meet Arnold at West Point. As the whole party were seated in the barge moving smoothly over the water, with the majestic scenery of the highlands about them, Washington said, "Well, gentlemen, I am glad, on the whole, that General Arnold has gone before us, for we shall now have a salute; and the roaring of the cannon will have a fine effect among these mountains." The boat drew near to the beach, but no cannon were heard, and there was no appearance of preparation to receive them. "What!" said Washington, "do they not intend to salute us!" At this moment an officer was seen making his way down the hill to meet them, who seemed confused at their arrival, and apologized for not being prepared to receive such distinguished visitors. "How is this, Sir," said Washington, "is not General Arnold here?" "No, Sir," replied the officer, "he has not been here these two days, nor have I heard from him within that time." "This is extraordinary," said Washington; "we were told he had crossed the river, and that we should find him here. However, our visit must not be in vain. Since we have come, we must look round a little, and see in what state things are with you." He then ascended the hill, examined Fort Putnam and the other fortifications, and returned to Arnold's house, where the treason was at once revealed. This had occupied two or three hours, however, and Arnold was beyond pursuit. Washington retained his usual calmness, though Arnold was one of his favourite officers, and had been placed at West Point by his own personal influence with Congress. He called Lafayette and Knox, showed them the proofs, and only said to the former, "Whom can we trust now!"

VIEW OF STATE STREET, BOSTON.

Boston is situated at the head of Massachusetts bay, on a peninsula about four miles in circumference, and is about three miles in length, and one mile and twenty-five rods, where widest, in breadth, and is connected with the main land at the south end by a narrow isthmus, called the Neck, leading to Roxbury. The town is built in an irregular circular form round the harbour, which is studded with about forty small islands, many of which afford excellent pasture; and are frequented in summer by numerous parties of pleasure. The harbour is formed by Nahant Point on the north, and Point Alderton on the south, and is so capacious as to allow five hundred vessels to ride at anchor in a good depth of water, while the entrance is so narrow as scarcely to admit two ships abreast. The entrance is defended by Fort Independence, belonging to the United States, on Castle Island, and by Fort Warren, on Governor's Island. There is another fort, called Fort Strong, on Noddle's Island.

Alterations and additions have of late years greatly improved the appearance of Boston. The streets, which were formerly almost without an exception narrow and crooked, have been in a great degree rendered wide and commodious; the old wooden structures have in the greater part of the city been replaced by handsome buildings of stone or brick. In the western part, particularly, there is much neatness and elegance. The splendour of the private buildings here, is not equalled in any other part of the Union.

The literary institutions of this city are of the first order. The public libraries contain 70,000 volumes. The Boston Athenæum is the finest establishment of its kind in the United States; its library contains above 25,000 volumes, and a reading-room, in which the most esteemed periodicals, from all parts of the world, may be found. If we add to these the library of Harvard College, in the neighbourhood, of 40,000 volumes, making the number of books within the reach of the citizens 110,000, it must be allowed that Boston offers to the scholar a more advantageous residence than any other spot in the western world.

State Street, called King Street in the days of Stamp-acts and "the Regulars," is the main artery of the heart of New England. The old State House, which stands at the head of it, was called the Town House, and was first erected in 1660. It is honourably mentioned in a book of travels, written in a pleasant vein, by "John Josselyn, Gent." who visited the colonies in 1663. "There is also a Town House," he says, "built upon pillars,

27

where the merchants may confer. In the chambers above they hold their monthly courts. Here is the dwelling of the Governor (Bellingham). On the south there is a small but pleasant common, where the gallants, a little before sunset, walk with their marmalet madams, as we do in Moorfields, till the nine o'clock bell rings them home to their respective habitations; when presently, the constables walk the rounds to see good order kept, and to take up loose people." The State House has been twice burnt, and rebuilt. A council chamber, ornamented with full-length portraits of Charles II. and James II. formerly occupied the east end; and it was in this chamber that James Otis declared before a court of admiralty, that "taxation without representation is tyranny,"—a phrase which became, before long, a slogan in the mouths of the people. "Then and there," writes President Adams, "was the first scene of the first act of opposition to the arbitrary claims of Great Britain. Then and there, the child Independence was born." It was upon a trial of the question of "Writs for Assistance," a power which was required by the Board of Trade to enforce some new and rigorous Acts of Parliament touching trade; and Otis opposed the Attorney-General. "As soon as he had concluded," says the historian, "Otis burst forth as with a flame of fire, with a promptitude of classical allusion, a depth of research, a rapid summary of historical events, a profusion of legal authorities, a prophetic glance into futurity, and a torrent of impetuous eloquence, which carried all before him." This was the preparation for the resistance to the Stamp Act, and the Revolution soon followed.

State Street has been the scene of most of the events of a very public nature, which are recorded in the annals of Boston. The balcony of the State House is the popular pulpit, and hence was read the Declaration of Independence, and from hence declaimed Colonel David Crockett, who "could lick his weight in wild-cats." In 1770 the "Boston massacre" took place in State Street. For several days preceding the event, there had been disturbances between the king's soldiers and the townspeople, which had put the officers on the alert. The soldiers were collected into the barracks before night, and sentinels were placed around them at all hours to prevent difficulty. One of these sentinels was stationed in a narrow alley, and was striking fire against the walls with his sword, for amusement, when two or three young men attempted to pass him. Having orders to let no one pass, a struggle ensued, and one of the young men received a wound on the head. The noise of the rencontre drew together a considerable crowd, and as but few could enter the narrow scene of action, the remainder listened to an inflammatory speech from "a tall man, with a red cloak, and a white wig," in the adjacent square. At the close of the oration there was a general cry "To the main guard!" and the crowd rushed tumultuously toward its station in State Street. On their way they passed the Custom House, before the door of which stood a single sentinel. Alarmed at their approach, he retreated up the steps, and, the people collecting around, he sent word to the barracks, near by, that he was attacked, and a company in a few moments arrived to his assistance, and formed a half circle round the steps. The captain of the day, named Preston, followed immediately, and the Custom House, which stood at the corner of State and Exchange Streets, was soon thronged by a considerable multitude. The soldiers were soon pressed upon very closely by the mob, who were mostly armed with clubs; and those at a distance soon began to throw snowballs, followed by fragments of ice, stones and sticks, while from every side came the cry, "Fire, if you dare!" The soldiers soon heard, or thought they heard, the order, and they fired in quick succession from right to left. Two or three of the guns flashed, but the rest were fatal. Three persons were killed on the spot, two received wounds of which they died next day, and others were more slightly injured. The people immediately dispersed, leaving the dead bodies in the street, but returned in a few minutes; when the soldiers aimed once more at them, but the commanding officer struck up the guns with his sword. The drum was beat to arms, and several of the officers, on their way to join the guard, were knocked down, and their swords taken from them. Order was soon restored, and Captain Preston delivered himself up for trial. The dead were buried with some pomp, and when the excitement had subsided a little, Preston was tried and acquitted.

State Street is at present a street of banks, insurance offices, and similar institutions; and its side walk serves for the merchants' exchange. The buildings are of granite, and some of them, particularly a new bank, lately erected near Kilby Street, present very creditable specimens of city architecture.

NIAGARA FALLS, FROM CLIFTON HOUSE.

The most comprehensive view of Niagara is, no doubt, that from the galleries of this hotel; but it is, at the same time, for a first view, one of the most unfavourable. Clifton House stands nearly opposite the centre of the irregular crescent formed by the Falls; but it is so far back from the line of the arc, that the height and grandeur of the two cataracts, to an eye unacquainted with the scene, are deceptively diminished. After once making the tour of the points of view, however, the distance and elevation of the hotel are allowed for by the eye, and the situation seems most advantageous. This is the only house at Niagara where a traveller, on his second visit, would be content to live.

Clifton House is kept in the best style of hotels in this country; but the usual routine of such places, going on in the very eye of Niagara, weaves in very whimsically with the eternal presence and power of the cataract. We must eat, drink, and sleep, it is true, at Niagara as elsewhere; and indeed, what with the exhaustion of mind and fatigue of body, we require at the Falls perhaps more than usual of these three "blessed inventions." The leaf that is caught away by the Rapids, however, is not more entirely possessed by this wonder of nature, than is the mind and imagination of the traveller; and the arrest of that leaf by the touch of the overhanging tree, or the point of a rock amid the breakers, is scarce more momentary than the interruption to the traveller's enchantment by the circumstances of daily life. He falls asleep with its surging thunders in his ear, and wakes—to wonder, for an instant, if his yesterday's astonishment was a dream. With the succeeding thought, his mind refills, like a mountain channel, whose torrent has been suspended by the frost, and he is overwhelmed with sensations that are almost painful, from the suddenness of their return. He rises and throws up his window, and there it flashes, and thunders, and agonizes—the same almighty miracle of grandeur for ever going on; and he turns and wonders—What the deuce can have become of his stockings! He slips on his dressing-gown, and commences his toilet. The glass stands in the window, and with his beard half achieved, he gets a glimpse of the foam-cloud rising majestically over the top of the mahogany frame. Almost persuaded, like Queen Christina at the fountains of St. Peter's, that a spectacle of such splendour is not intended to last, he drops his razor, and with the soap drying unheeded on his chin, he leans on his elbows, and watches the yeasty writhe in the abysm, and the solemn pillars of crystal eternally falling, like the fragments of some palace-crested star, descending through interminable space. The white field of the iris forms over the brow of the cataract, exhibits its radiant bow, and sails away in a vanishing cloud of vapour upon the wind; the tortured and convulsed surface of the caldron below shoots out its frothy and seething circles in perpetual torment; the thunders are heaped upon each other, the earth trembles, and—the bell rings for breakfast! A vision of cold rolls, clammy omelettes, and tepid tea, succeeds these sublime images, and the traveller completes his toilet. Breakfast over, he resorts to the colonnade, to contemplate untiringly the scene before him, and in the midst of a calculation of the progress of the Fall towards Lake Erie,—with the perspiration standing on his forehead, while he struggles to conceive the junction of its waters with Lake Ontario,—the rocks rent, the hills swept away, forests prostrated, and the islands uprooted in the mighty conflux,—some one's child escapes from its nurse, and seizing him by the legs, cries out "Da-da."

The ennui attendant upon public-houses can never be felt at Clifton House. The most common mind finds the spectacle from its balconies a sufficient and untiring occupation. The loneliness of uninhabited parlours, the discord of baby-thrummed pianos, the dreariness of great staircases, long entries, and bar-rooms filled with strangers, are pains and penalties of travel never felt at Niagara. If there is a vacant half-hour to dinner, or if indisposition to sleep create that sickening yearning for society, which sometimes comes upon a stranger in a strange land, like the calenture of a fever,—the eternal marvel going on without is more engrossing than friend or conversation, more beguiling from sad thought than the Corso in carnival-time. To lean over the balustrade and watch the flying of the ferry-boat below, with its terrified freight of adventurers, one moment gliding swiftly down the stream in the round of an eddy, the next, lifted up by a boiling wave, as if it were tossed up from the scoop of a giant's hand beneath the water; to gaze hour after hour into the face of the cataract, to trace the rainbows, delight like a child in the shooting spray-clouds, and calculate fruitlessly and endlessly by the force, weight, speed, and change of the tremendous waters,—is amusement and occupation enough to draw the mind from any thing,—to cure madness or create it.

VIEW FROM HYDE PARK.

The Hudson at Hyde Park is a broad, tranquil, and noble river, of about the same character as the Bosphorus above Roumeli-bissar, or the Dardanelles at Abydos. The shores are cultivated to the water's edge, and lean up in graceful, rather than bold elevations; the eminences around are crested with the villas of the wealthy inhabitants of the metropolis at the river's mouth; summer-houses, belvideres, and water-steps, give an air of enjoyment and refreshment to the banks, and, without any thing like the degree of the picturesque which makes the river so remarkable thirty or forty miles below, it is, perhaps, a more tempting character of scenery to build and live among.

All along, in this part of the river, occur the "landings," which are either considerable towns in themselves, or indicate a thickly settled country in the rear. The immense steamers that ply on the Hudson leave and receive passengers at all these points, and, to a person making the passage for the first time, the manner and expedition of this operation is rather startling. In the summer time, the principal steam boats average from five to seven hundred passengers, and there is usually a considerable number to go ashore and come off at each place. A mile or two before reaching the spot, a negro makes the tour of the boat, with a large hand-bell, and, in an amusing speech, full of the idioms of his own race, announces the approach, and requests those who are going ashore to select their baggage. This done, the steamer, gliding over the smooth water at the rate of fifteen or twenty miles in the hour, sheers in toward the shore, and the small boat is lowered, with the captain in her at the helm; the passengers are put on board, and away she shoots at the end of a line gradually loosened, but still kept tight enough to send her, like an arrow to her mark. The moment she touches the pier, the loose line is let out from the steamer, which still keeps on her way, and between that moment and the exhaustion of the line, perhaps thirty seconds, the baggage is thrown out, and taken in, passengers jump ashore, and embark, and away shoots the little boat again, her bow rising clear over the crest of her own foam, with the added velocity of the steamer at full speed, and the rapid hauling in of the crew. I never have failed to observe a look of astonishment on the part of the subjects of this hurried transfer, however used to it by frequent repetition; and a long sigh of relief, as they look about on the broad and steady deck, or tread the ground beneath them if they have gone ashore, follows as invariably. As the boat is hauled up again, the negro crier reappears with his bell, and, looking the newly arrived group close in the face, cries out, as if they were a mile off, "All pas'ng'rs as hasn't paid their passage, please walk to the cap'n's office and settle-e-e!!"—the whole sentence recited in the most monotonous tone till the last syllable, which rises suddenly to a ludicrous scream, prolonged as long as his breath will continue it.

Many fatal accidents occurred formerly from this practice; but there is now more care and time taken about it, and the accidents, if any, are rather ludicrous than serious. I was going to Albany, some years ago, on board a very crowded boat, and among the passengers were a German and his wife, emigrants of the lower class. They had been down stairs at dinner, and the husband came up in search of his wife, who had preceded him, just as a crowded boatful were going ashore at Poughkeepsie. Either fancying it the end of his journey, or misunderstanding the man who was busy with the baggage, he threw in his bundle, and was peeping through the crowd of ladies on the stern for his wife; when one of the men, impatient of his delay, drew him in, and away he flew to the pier. He sprang ashore with the rest, his bundle was thrown after him, and, as the steamer sped away, we saw him darting about in the crowd to find his vrouw, who by this time had missed him, and was running from side to side, in quite as great embarrassment on board. The poor woman's distress was quite pitiable, and when, at last, one of the passengers, who had observed them together, pointed out to her her husband, in his flat cap and foreign bleuse, standing on the receding pier, with his hands stretched out after the boat, her agony could no longer be controlled. She was put ashore at the next landing to return by the "down boat;" but as another boat up the river arrived soon after at Poughkeepsie, the probability was, that he would embark again to follow her, and they would thus cross each other by the way; with scarce a word of English, and probably very little money, they may be hunting each other to this day.

VILLAGE OF SING-SING.

Sing-Sing is famous for its marble, of which there is an extensive quarry near by; for its State prison, of which the discipline is of the most salutary character; and for its academy, which has a high reputation. It may be said, altogether, to do the State some service.

The county of West Chester, of which this is the principal village on the Hudson, has been made the scene of, perhaps, the best historical novel of our country, and, more than any other part of the United States, suffered from the evils of war. The character and depredations of the "cow-boys" and "skinners," whose fields of action were on the skirts of this neutral ground, are familiar to all who have read "the Essay" of Mr. Cooper. A distinguished clergyman gives the following very graphic picture of West Chester county in those days:—

"In the autumn of 1777, I resided for some time in this county. The lines of the British were then in the neighbourhood of Kingsbridge, and those of the Americans at Byram river. The unhappy inhabitants were, therefore, exposed to the depredations of both. Often they were actually plundered, and always were liable to this calamity. They feared every body whom they saw, and loved nobody. It was a curious fact to a philosopher, and a melancholy one to hear their conversation. To every question they gave such an answer as would please the inquirer; or, if they despaired of pleasing, such a one as would not provoke him. Fear was, apparently, the only passion by which they were animated. The power of volition seemed to have deserted them. They were not civil, but obsequious; not obliging, but subservient. They yielded with a kind of apathy, and very quietly, what you asked, and what they supposed it impossible for them to retain. If you treated them kindly, they received it coldly; not as a kindness, but as a compensation for injuries done them by others. When you spoke to them, they answered you without either good or ill nature, and without any appearance of reluctance or hesitation; but they subjoined neither questions nor remarks of their own; proving to your full conviction that they felt no interest either in the conversation or yourself. Both their countenances and their motions had lost every trace of animation and of feeling. Their features were smoothed, not into serenity, but apathy; and, instead of being settled in the attitude of quiet thinking, strongly indicated, that all thought beyond what was merely instinctive, had fled their minds for ever.

"Their houses, meantime, were, in a great measure, scenes of desolation. Their furniture was extensively plundered, or broken to pieces. The walls, floors, and windows were injured both by violence and decay, and were not repaired, because they had not the means to repair them, and because they were exposed to the repetition of the same injuries. Their cattle were gone. Their enclosures were burnt, where they were capable of becoming fuel; and in many cases thrown down where they were not. Their fields were covered with a rank growth of weeds and wild grass.

"Amid all this appearance of desolation, nothing struck my eye more forcibly than the sight of the high road. Where I had heretofore seen a continual succession of horses and carriages, life and bustle lending a sprightliness to all the environing objects, not a single, solitary traveller was seen, from week to week, or from month to month. The world was motionless and silent, except when one of these unhappy people ventured upon a rare and lonely excursion to the house of a neighbour no less unhappy, or a scouting party, traversing the country in quest of enemies, alarmed the inhabitants with expectations of new injuries and sufferings. The very tracks of the carriages were grown over, and obliterated; and where they were discernible, resembled the faint impressions of chariot wheels, said to be left on the pavements of Herculaneum. The grass was of full height for the scythe, and strongly realized to my own mind, for the first time, the proper import of that picturesque declaration in the Song of Deborah: 'In the days of Shamgar, the son of Anath, in the days of Jael, the highways were unoccupied, and the travellers walked through by-paths. The inhabitants of the villages ceased: they ceased in Israel.' "

West Chester is a rough county in natural surface, but since the days when the above description was true, its vicinity to New York, and the ready market for produce, have changed its character to a thriving agricultural district. It is better watered with springs, brooks, and mill-streams, than many other parts of New York, and, among other advantages, enjoys, along the Hudson, a succession of brilliant and noble scenery.

VIEW FROM RUGGLE'S HOUSE, NEWBURGH, HUDSON RIVER.
Newburgh stands upon a pretty acclivity, rising with a sharp ascent from the east bank of the Hudson; and, in point of trade and consequence, it is one of the first towns on the river. In point of scenery, Newburgh is as felicitously placed, perhaps, as any other spot in the world, having in its immediate neighbourhood every element of natural loveliness; and, just below, the sublime and promising Pass of the Highlands. From the summit of the acclivity, the view over Wateaman and Fishkill is full of beauty; the deep flow of the Hudson lying between, and the pretty villages just named, sparkling with their white buildings and cheerful steeples, beyond.

32

Newburgh has a considerable trade with the back country, and supports two or three steam-boats, running daily and exclusively between its pier and New York. If there were wanting an index of the wondrous advance of enterprise and invention in our country, we need not seek farther than this simple fact—a small intermediate town, on one river, supporting such an amount of expensive navigation. Only thirty years ago Fulton made his first experiment in steam on the Hudson, amid the unbelief and derision of the whole country. Let any one stand for one hour on the pier at Newburgh, and see those superb and swift palaces of motion shoot past, one after the other, like gay and chasing meteors; and then read poor Fulton's account of his first experiment—and never again throw discouragement on the kindling fire of genius.

"When I was building my first steam-boat," said he to Judge Story, "the project was viewed by the public at New York either with indifference or contempt, as a visionary scheme. My friends, indeed, were civil, but they were shy. They listened with patience to my explanations, but with a settled cast of incredulity on their countenances. I felt the full force of the lamentation of the Poet:—

'Truths would you teach, to save a sinking land,
All shun, none aid you, and few understand.'

As I had occasion to pass daily to and from the building-yard while my boat was in progress, I have often loitered, unknown, near the idle groups of strangers gathering in little circles, and heard various inquiries as to the object of this new vehicle. The language was uniformly that of scorn, sneer, or ridicule. The loud laugh rose at my expense; the dry jest, the wise calculation of losses and expenditure; the dull but endless repetition of "the Fulton folly." Never did a single encouraging remark, a bright hope, or a warm wish, cross my path.

"At length the day arrived when the experiment was to be made. To me it was a most trying and interesting occasion. I wanted many friends to go on board to witness the first successful trip. Many of them did me the favour to attend, as a matter of personal respect; but it was manifest they did it with reluctance, feigning to be partners of my mortification, and not of my triumph. I was well aware that, in my case, there were many reasons to doubt of my own success. The machinery was new, and ill-made; and many parts of it were constructed by mechanics unacquainted with such work; and unexpected difficulties might reasonably be presumed to present themselves from other causes. The moment arrived in which the word was to be given for the vessel to move. My friends were in groups on the deck. There was anxiety mixed with fear among them. They were silent, sad, and weary. I read in their looks nothing but disaster, and almost repented of my efforts. The signal was given, and the boat moved on a short distance, and then stopped, and became immovable. To the silence of the preceding moment, now succeeded murmurs of discontent and agitation, and whispers and shrugs. I could hear distinctly repeated, "I told you so,—it is a foolish scheme.—I wish we were well out of it." I elevated myself on a platform, and stated that I knew not what was the matter; but if they would be quiet, and indulge me for half an hour, I would either go on or abandon the voyage. I went below, and discovered that a slight maladjustment was the cause. It was obviated. The boat went on; we left New York; we passed through the Highlands; we reached Albany!—Yet even then, imagination superseded the force of fact. It was doubted if it could be done again, or if it could be made, in any case, of any great value."

What an affecting picture of the struggles of a great mind, and what a vivid lesson of encouragement to genius, is contained in this simple narration!

DESCENT INTO THE VALLEY OF WYOMING.

In looking down on this lovely scene, made memorable by savage barbarity, and famous by the poet's wand of enchantment, it is natural to indulge in resentful feelings towards the sanguinary race whose atrocities make up its page in story. It is a pity, however, that they too, had not a poet and a partial chronicler. Leaving entirely out of view the ten thousand wrongs done by the white man to the Indian, in the corruption, robbery, and rapid extinction of his race, there are personal atrocities, on our own records, exercised toward that fated people, which, in impartial history hereafter, will redeem them from all charge except that of irresistible retaliation. The brief story of the famous Cornstalk, Sachem of the Shawanees, and King of the Northern Confederacy, is sermon enough on this text.

The north-western corner of Virginia, and that part of Pennsylvania contiguous, on the south, to the valley represented in the drawing, was the scene of some of the bloodiest events of Indian warfare. Distinguished over all the other red men of this region, was Cornstalk. He was equally a terror to the men of his own tribe, (whom he did not hesitate to hew down with his tomahawk if they showed any cowardice in fight,) and a formidable opponent to our troops, from his military talents and personal daring. He was, at the same time, more than all the other chiefs of the confederacy, a friend to the whites; and, energetic as he was when once engaged in battle, never took up arms willingly against them. After the bloody contest at Point Pleasant, in which Cornstalk had displayed his generalship and bravery, to the admiration of his foes, he came in to the camp of Lord Dunmore, to make negotiations for peace. Colonel Wilson, one of the staff, thus describes his oratory:—"When he arose, he was in no wise confused or daunted, but spoke in a distinct and audible voice, without stammering or repetition, and with peculiar emphasis. His looks, while addressing Dunmore, were truly grand and majestic, yet graceful and attractive. I have heard many celebrated orators, but never one whose powers of delivery surpassed those of Cornstalk on this occasion."

In the spring of 1777, it was known that an extensive coalition was forming among the tribes, and that it only waited the consent and powerful aid of the Shawanees, to commence war upon the whites. At this critical time, Cornstalk, accompanied by Red Hawk, came on a friendly visit to the Fort at Point Pleasant, communicated the intentions of the tribes, and expressed his sorrow that the tide set so strongly against the colonists, that he must go with it, in spite of all his endeavours.

Upon receiving this information, given by the noble savage in the spirit of a generous enemy, the commander of the garrison seized upon Cornstalk and his companion as hostages for the peaceful conduct of his nation, and set about availing himself of the advantage he had gained by his suggestions. During his captivity, Cornstalk held frequent conversations with the officers, and took pleasure in describing to them the geography of the west, then little known. One afternoon, while he was engaged in drawing on the floor a map of the Missouri territory, with its water-courses and mountains, a halloo was heard from the forest, which he recognised as the voice of his son Ellinipsico, a young warrior, whose courage and address was almost as celebrated as his own. Ellinipsico entered the fort, and embraced his father most affectionately, having been uneasy at his long absence, and come hither in search of him.

The day after his arrival, a soldier went out from the fort on a hunting excursion, and was shot by Indians. His infuriated companions instantly resolved to sacrifice Cornstalk and his son. They charged upon Ellinipsico that the offenders were in his company, but he declared that he had come alone, and with the sole object of seeking his father. When the soldiers came within hearing, the young warrior appeared agitated. Cornstalk encouraged him to meet his fate composedly, and said to him, "My son, the

34

Great Spirit has sent you here that we may die together!" He turned to meet his murderers the next instant, and receiving seven bullets in his body, expired without a groan.

When Cornstalk had fallen, Ellinipsico continued still and passive, not even raising himself from his seat. He met death in that position with the utmost calmness. "The other Indian," says the chronicle, "was murdered piecemeal, and with all those circumstances of cruelty with which the savage wreaks his vengeance on his enemy."

The day before his death, Cornstalk been present at a council of the officers, and had spoken to them on the subject of the war, with his own peculiar eloquence. In the course of his remarks, he expressed something like a presentiment of his fate. "When I was young," he said, "and went out to war, I often thought each would be my last adventure, and I should return no more. I still lived. Now I am in the midst of you, and, if you choose, you may kill me. I can die but once. It is alike to me whether now or hereafter!"

His atrocious murder was dearly expiated. The Shawanees, the most warlike tribe of the West, became thenceforward the most deadly and implacable foes to the white man.

BOSTON, FROM DORCHESTER HEIGHTS.

The pretty peninsula of Dorchester Heights, which seems to throw its arm protectingly around the southern bay of Boston, was settled by a company of pilgrims who came out to New England during the administration of Governor Winthrop, in Massachusetts. The party consisted of two Puritan clergymen, "with many godly families and people" from Devonshire and Somersetshire, who embarked in the "Mary John," in the spring of 1630. The historian states that they had some difficulty in the passage with the master of the vessel, Captain Squibb, "who, like a merciless man, put them and their goods ashore on Nantasket Point, notwithstanding his engagement was to bring them up Charles river." They obtained a boat, however, and, having laden her with goods, and manned her with able men ("not more than ten, well armed, under Captain Southcot, a brave Low-country soldier,") they followed the river for about ten miles. After landing their goods on a steep bank, they were alarmed by the information that there was encamped near them a body of three hundred savages. Fortunately they had been joined by an old planter, who knew enough of the Indian tongue and disposition to persuade the chiefs not to attack the party till morning. At day-break, some of the savages made their appearance, but stood awhile at a distance. At last one of them held out a bass, and the pilgrims sent a man with a biscuit to exchange for it, and thus a friendly intercourse was established. Not liking the neighbourhood, however, they descended the river again, and an exploring party having discovered some good pasture at Mattapau (present Dorchester) they settled there.

The neighbouring peninsula of Shawmut (now Boston) was destined to be the principal settlement, and Dorchester is at this day a rural suburb of the capital of New England. The fort which crowns its summit (from which this view is taken) is the scene of an important chapter in the history of the Revolution.

Boston had been occupied for some time by the British army under General Gage, who sailed for England in October 1776, leaving General Howe in command. After the battle of Bunker's Hill, both armies remained quiet for several months; General Washington occupying both sides of the Charles river with about fourteen thousand men; and the English, besieged in their quarters within the town, amusing themselves with private theatricals in Faneuiel Hall, varied occasionally with feats of horsemanship from a squadron of cavalry, who had turned the old South Church into a circus. As the cold became severe, the North "meeting-house," an immense wooden building, was torn down and consumed for fuel, and the soldiers had made a holiday of felling a gigantic Liberty-tree for the same purpose.

Washington became impatient of this inactive situation; and as soon as the ice in the bay and river became firm enough to allow the passage of troops, he called a council of war, and proposed an attack on Boston. The opinion against the measure was unanimous, and he reluctantly abandoned it. He soon after determined to take possession of Dorchester Heights, which command both harbour and town,—a step which he knew must bring on a general action, during which he intended to cross over to Cambridge with a few chosen men, and force an entrance into the town. During the two or three preceding nights, he bombarded the town heavily from his camp, to divert the attention of the garrison; and on the night of the 4th of March, a large detachment took possession of Dorchester Heights, and immediately commenced throwing up an intrenchment. The night was mild, but the ground was frozen almost impenetrably hard; and it was with excessive labour that a sufficient bulwark was presented by day-light, to cover them from the shot of the enemy.

The morning broke,—and a thin haze, which magnified the size of the works, overspread the landscape. The astonishment of General Howe, at discerning this phantom fortification looming up through the mist, upon heights which had been bare and desolate at sunset, was without bounds. The position was so commanding that the town could not be held unless the Americans were dislodged; but this seemed, from the advantages of the ground in favour of the Provincials, next to impossible. The British commander undertook it with great spirit, and two thousand troops were embarked on the same day to cross the harbour to the attack. The transports fell down to the Castle, a small island just below the town; but a tremendous storm suspended their operations. The next day a council of war was held, and it was thought advisable to evacuate the town immediately. The provincials went on completing their fortifications, undisturbed; and in a few days General Howe embarked with all his forces, accompanied by those Americans who adhered to the royal cause. The embarkation commenced at four in the morning of the 17th of March, and at ten in the forenoon General Washington entered the city at the head of his army. The English fleet sailed for Halifax. They were ten thousand strong, including the marines; and left stores to the value of 30,000l. with several pieces of cannon, mortars, &c. &c.

The view of Boston from these heights is very commanding. The bay, with its fortified islands, stretches away to the right, beautiful from its shape and from the brightness of its water; the city, clustering upon its heights, rises in graceful lines to the pinnacled State House; and the country to the left is all that is lovely in cultivation, sprinkled here and there with gay and thrifty-looking villages. The calenture of speculation is just now at its height in America; and Dorchester, like other places, is laid out in lots, and busy with the builders of fancy cottages and hotels. If calculation has not overreached itself, the suburbs of Boston will soon sparkle with villas on every hill side within the horizon.

VIEW OF FANEUIL HALL, AND ADJACENT BUILDINGS, BOSTON.

There are very few remaining of the many covered, gable-ended, top-heavy, old houses which constituted the compact centre of Boston in the days of English governors. The finest specimens long stood in the neighbourhood of Faneuiel Hall; but, with one exception, we believe, their picturesque heaps of triangles have dropped beneath the merciless hand of speculation and improvement. Boston has not grown so thriftily, or rather so miraculously, as the capitols of other States, through which the flood of emigration rolls more directly; but it is certainly the handsomest town in the United States, and probably its prosperity is more permanent and solid. Its granite houses and fine public buildings are in strong contrast with the description given of it by John Josselyn, Gent. who visited it in 1638, and afterwards favoured the world with his observations under the title of "New England Rarities." "Having refreshed myself for a day or two on an island in the bay," he says, "I crossed the harbour in a small boat to Boston, which was then rather a village than a town, there not being more than above twenty or thirty houses: and presented my respects to Mr. Muthrop the governor, and to Mr. Cotton the teacher of Boston Church, to whom I delivered from Mr. Francis Quarles, the poet, the translation of several Psalms in English metre for his approbation."

A facetious bookseller, John Dunton, visited Boston some fifty years afterwards; and, in a book upon his "Life and Errors," gives a humorous account of its inhabitants in his time. The passage, which is now commonly made in from sixteen to twenty-five or thirty days, occupied the unfortunate bibliopole four months; and he was reduced, at the latter part of it, to one bottle of water for four days.

"When we came within view of Boston," he writes, "we were all overjoyed, being just upon the point of starving; we put off to land in the long boat, and came ashore near the Castle, which stands about a mile from Boston. The country appeared at first a barren waste, but we found humanity enough when we came among the inhabitants. We lodged the first night at the Castle, and next morning we found our way to Boston Bay over the ice, which was but cold comfort to us after we had been stowed up so many months in a cabin. The air of New England was sharper than at London; which, with the temptation of fresh provisions, made me eat like a second Mariot of Gray's Inn. The first person that welcomed me to Boston was Mr. Burroughs. He heaped upon me more civilities than I can reckon up, offered to lend me moneys, and made me his bedfellow till I had provided lodgings."

Dunton's book would have sold merrily in our scandal-loving days. Its personalities are delightful. The following list of his acquaintance is as good as a portrait gallery.

"Mr. Phillips, my old correspondent.—He treated me with a noble dinner, and (if I may trust my eyes) is blest with a pretty, obliging wife. I'll say that for Sam (after dealing with him for some hundred pounds), he is very just, and (as an effect of that) very thriving. I shall add to his character, that he is young and witty, and the most beautiful man in the town of Boston.

"The next was Mr. King.—Love was the cause of this gentleman's long ramble hither. Sure his mistress was made of stone, for King had a voice would have charmed the spheres; he sang "All hail to the Myrtle Shades" with a matchless grace.

"Another acquaintance was Mr. York. He had his soft minutes as well as other men; and when he unbent his bow, (for he was very industrious,) he treated the fair sex with so much courtship and address, as if loving had been all his trade.

"I pass to my good friend Dr. Bullivant—both a gentleman and a physician. As a gentleman, he came of noble family, but his good qualities exceed his birth. He never practises new experiments on his patients, except in dangerous cases, where death must be expelled by death. This is also praiseworthy in him, that to the poor he always prescribes cheap medicines; not curing them of a consumption in their bodies and sending it into their purses, nor yet directing them to the East Indies for drugs, when they may have better out of their own gardens.

"I proceed in the next place to Mr. Gouge, a linen-draper from London. He is owner of a deal of wit; his brain is a quiver of smart jests. He pretends to live a bachelor, but is no enemy to a pretty woman."

Dunton winds up his list with an apostrophe to Mrs. Comfort, the married daughter of his landlady. "You may well take it amiss," he says, "if I should forget your favours to me in your father's house, your pleasant company to Ipswich, your assistance when I was ill, and the noble looking-glass you sent my dear, and all with a world of innocence."

"Kind Boston, adieu! part we must, though 'tis pity,
But I'm made for mankind: the world is my city.
Look how on the shore they whoop and they holloa,
Not for joy I am gone, but for grief they can't follow."

VIEW FROM THE TELEGRAPH SIGNAL, NEW YORK BAY.

The first visitor to the Bay of New York, and the writer of the first description on record, was John de Verrazzano, a Florentine, in the service of Francis the First. This bold navigator had been for some time in command of four ships, cruising against the Spaniards. But his little fleet being separated in a storm, Verrazzano determined, with one of them, the Dauphin, to take a voyage in search of new countries. He arrived on the American coast, somewhere near North Carolina, and first proceeded south as far as "the region of palm-trees," probably Florida. He then turned, and proceeded north till he entered a harbour, which he describes thus, in a passage of a letter addressed by him to his Royal master:—

"This land is situated in the paralele of Rome, in forty-one degrees and two terces; but somewhat more colde by accidentall causes. The mouth of the haven lieth open to the south, half a league broad; and being entred within it, between the east and the north, it stretcheth twelve leagues, where it wareth broader and broader, and maketh a gulfe about twenty leagues in compass, wherein are five small islands, very fruitfull and pleasant, full of hie and broad trees, among the which islands any great navie may ride safe without any feare of tempest or other danger."

In this harbour Verrazzano appears to have remained about fifteen days. He and his men frequently went on shore to obtain supplies and see the country. He says in another part of his letter—"Sometimes our men stayed two or three daies on a little island neere the ship for divers necessaries. We were oftentimes within the land five or six leagues, which we found as pleasant as is possible to declare, very apt for any kind of husbandry, of corne, wine, and ayle. We entered afterwards into the woods, which we found so thicke that any army, were it never so great, might have hid itself therein; the trees whereof are okes, cypresse-trees, and other sortes unknown in Europe."

These were probably the first European feet that ever trod on any part of the territory now included in the State of New York. Verrazzano and his crew seem to have had considerable intercourse with the natives, and generally to have been treated well, though by his own account he did not always deserve it. Speaking of an excursion made by his men somewhere on the coast, he says:—"They saw only one old woman, with a young maid of eighteen or twenty yeeres old, which, seeing our companie, hid themselves in the grasse for feare. The old woman carried two infants on her shoulders, and the young woman was laden with as many. As soone as they saw us, to quiet them and win their favours, our men gave them victuals to eate, which the old woman received thankfully, but the young woman threw them disdainfully on the ground. They took a child from the old woman to bring into France; and going about to take the young woman, which was very beautiful, and of tall stature, they could not possibly, for the great outcries that she made, bring her to the sea; and especially having great woods to pass thorow, and being far from the ship, we proposed to leave her behind, bearing away the child only."

In a subsequent part of his narrative, Verrazzano presents a very favourable picture, not only of the amenity, but of the discretion of the aborigines. "They came in great companies of their small boats unto the ship, with their faces all bepainted with divers colours, and bringing their wives with them, whereof they were very jealous; they themselves entring aboard the ship, and staying there a good space, but causing their wives to stay in their boats; and for all the entreatie that we could make, offering to give them divers things, we could never obtaine that they would suffer them to come aboard the ship. And oftentimes one of the two Kings comming with his Queene, and many gentlemen for their pleasure to see us, they all stayed on shore 200 paces from us, sending us a small boat to give us intelligence of their comming; and as soon as they had answere from us they came immediately, and wondered at hearing the cries and noyses of the mariners. The Queene and her maids staied in a very light boat at an island a quarter of a league off, while the King abode a long space in our ship, uttering divers conceits with gestures, viewing with great admiration the furniture of the shippe. And sometimes our men staying one or two days on a little island near the ship, he returned with seven or eight of his gentlemen to see what we did; then the King drawing his bow, and running up and down with his gentlemen, made much sport to gratify our men."

The sail-studded bay of New York at this day presents another scene; and one of these same "gentlemen" is now almost as much a curiosity here as was John de Verrazano, only three centuries ago, to the rightful lords of this fair land and water.

PEEKSKILL LANDING.

Like most of the landings on the Hudson, Peekskill is a sort of outstretched hand from the interior of the country. It is about eighty miles from New York, and the produce from the country behind is here handed over to the trading sloops, who return, into the waiting palm, the equivalent in goods from the city. A sort of town naturally springs up at such a spot, and, as a river-side is a great provocative of idleness, all the Dolph Heyligers of the country about seem to be collected at the landing.

The neighbourhood of this spot is interesting from its association with the history of the Revolution. The head-quarters of General Washington were just below, at Verplank's Point; and the town of Peekskill, half a mile back from the river, was the depôt of military stores, which were burnt by General Home in 1777. "On my return southward in 1782," says the translator of Chastellux, who has not given his name, "I spent a day or two at the American camp at Verplank's Point, where I had the honour of dining with General Washington. I had suffered severely from an ague, which I could not get quit of, though I had taken the exercise of a hard-trotting horse, and got thus far to the north in the month of October. The General observing it, told me he was sure I had not met with a good glass of wine for some time,—an article then very rare,—but that my disorder must be frightened away. He make me drink three or four of his silver camp cups of excellent Madeira at noon, and recommended to me to take a generous glass of claret after dinner; a prescription by no means repugnant to my feelings, and which I most religiously followed. I mounted my horse the next morning, and continued my journey to Massachusetts, without ever experiencing the slightest return of my disorder.

"The American camp here presented the most beautiful and picturesque appearance. It extended along the plain, on the neck of land formed by the winding of the Hudson, and had a view of this river to the south. Behind it, the lofty mountains, covered with

39

wood, formed the most sublime back-ground that painting could express. In the front of the tents was a regular continued portico, formed by the boughs of the trees in full verdure, decorated with much taste and fancy. Opposite the camp, and on distinct eminences, stood the tents of some of the general officers, over which towered predominant that of Washington. I had seen all the camps in England, from many of which drawings and engravings have been taken; but this was truly a subject worthy the pencil of the first artist. The French camp, during their stay in Baltimore, was decorated in the same manner. At the camp at Verplank's Point we distinctly heard the morning and evening gun of the British at Knightsbridge."

The curiosity seizes with avidity upon any accidental information which fills up the bare outline of history. The personal history of Washington more particularly, wherever it has been traced by those who were in contact with him, is full of interest. Some of the sketches given by the Marquis of Chastellux, who passed this point of the Hudson on his way to Washington's head-quarters below, are very graphic.

"The weather being fair on the 26th," he says, "I got on horseback, after breakfasting with the General. He was so attentive as to give me the horse I rode on the day of my arrival. I found him as good as he is handsome; but, above all, perfectly well broke and well trained, having a good mouth, easy in hand, and stopping short in a gallop without bearing the bit. I mention these minute particulars, because it is the General himself who breaks all his own horses. He is an excellent and bold horseman, leaping the highest fences, and going extremely quick without standing upon his stirrups, bearing on the bridle, or letting his horse run wild; circumstances which our young men look upon as so essential a part of English horsemanship, that they would rather break a leg or an arm than renounce them."

After passing some days at head-quarters, this young nobleman thus admirably sums up his observations on Washington:—

"The strongest characteristic of this great man is the perfect union which reigns between his physical and moral qualities. Brave without temerity, laborious without ambition, generous without prodigality, noble without pride, virtuous without severity; he seems always to have confined himself within those limits beyond which the virtues, by clothing themselves in more lively but more changeable colours, may be mistaken for faults. It will be said of him hereafter, that at the end of a long civil war he had nothing with which he could reproach himself. His stature is noble and lofty, he is well made and exactly proportioned; his physiognomy mild and agreeable, but such as to render it impossible to speak particularly of any of his features; so that on quitting him, you have only the recollection of a fine face. He has neither a grave nor a familiar air; his brow is sometimes marked with thought, but never with inquietude; in inspiring respect he inspires confidence, and his smile is always the smile of benevolence."

LIGHTHOUSE NEAR CALDWELL'S LANDING.

This picturesque object is seen to great effect by the passenger in the evening boat from New York to Newburgh. Leaving the city at five in the summer afternoon, she makes the intervening forty miles between that hour and twilight; and while the last tints of the sunset are still in the sky, the stars just beginning to twinkle through the glow of the west, the bright light of this lofty beacon rises up over the prow of the boat, shining apparently on the very face of the new-starred heaven. As he approaches, across the smooth and still purpled mirror of the silent river is drawn a long and slender line of light, broken at the foot of the beacon by the mild shrubbery of the rock on which it stands; and as he rounds the point, and passes it, the light brightens and looks clearer against the darker sky of the east, while the same cheering line of reflection follows him on his way, and is lost to sight as he disappears among the mountains.

The waters of the river at this point were the scene of the brief and tragic drama enacted so fatally by poor André. Four or five miles below stands Smith's house, where he had his principal interview with Arnold, and where the latter communicated to him his plans for the delivery of West Point into the hands of the English, and gave him the fatal papers which proved his ruin.

At Smith's house Mrs. Arnold passed a night, on her way to join her husband at West Point, soon after he had taken command. The sufferings of this lady have excited the sympathy of the world, as the first paroxysms of her distress moved the kind but firm heart of Washington. There seems to have arisen a doubt, however, whether her long and well-known correspondence with André had not so far undermined her patriotism, that she was rather inclined to further than impede the treason of Arnold; and consequently could have suffered but little after Washington generously made every arrangement for her to follow him. In the "Life of Aaron Burr," lately published, are some statements which seem authentic on the subject. It is well known that Washington found Mrs. Arnold apparently frantic with distress at the communication her husband had made to her the moment before his flight. Lafayette, and the other officers in the suite of the commander-in-chief, were alive with the most poignant sympathy; and a passport was given her by Washington, with which she immediately left West Point to join Arnold in New York. On her way she stopped at the house of Mrs. Prevost, the wife of a British officer, who subsequently married Colonel Burr. Here "the frantic scenes of West Point were renewed," says the narrative of Burr's biographer, "and continued so long as strangers were present. As soon as she and Mrs. Prevost were left alone, however, Mrs. Arnold became tranquillized, and assured Mrs. Prevost that she was heartily sick of the theatrics she was exhibiting. She stated that she had corresponded with the British commander; that she was disgusted with the American cause, and those who had the management of public affairs; and that, through great persuasion and unceasing perseverance, she had ultimately brought the General into an arrangement to surrender West Point to the British. Mrs. Arnold was a gay, accomplished, artful, and extravagant woman. There is no doubt, therefore, that, for the purpose of acquiring the means of gratifying her vanity, she contributed greatly to the utter ruin of her husband, and thus doomed to everlasting infamy and disgrace all the fame he had acquired as a gallant soldier, at the sacrifice of his blood."

It is not easy to pass and repass the now peaceful and beautiful waters of this part of the Hudson, without recalling to mind the scenes and actors in the great drama of the revolution, which they not long ago bore on their bosom. The busy mind fancies the armed guard-boats, slowly pulling along the shore; the light pinnace of the Vulture plying to and fro on its errands of conspiracy; and not the least vivid picture to the imagination, is the boat containing the accomplished, the gallant André and his guard, on his way to his death. It is probable that he first admitted to his own mind the possibility of a fatal result, while passing the very spot presented in the drawing. A late biographer of Arnold gives the particulars of a conversation between André and Major Tallmadge, the officer who had him in custody, and who brought him from West Point down the river to Tuppau, the place of his subsequent execution.

"Before we reached the Clove" (a landing just below the beacon represented in the drawing,) "Major André became very inquisitive to know my opinion as to the result of his capture. When I could no longer evade his importunity, I remarked to him as follows:—'I had a much-loved classmate in Yale College, by the name of Hale, who entered the army in 1775. Immediately after the battle of Long Island, Washington wanted information respecting the strength of the enemy. Hale tendered his services, went over to Brooklyn, and was taken, just as he was passing the outposts of the enemy on his return.' Said I, with emphasis, 'Do you remember the sequel of this story?' 'Yes,' said André, 'he was hanged as a spy. But you surely do not consider his case and mine alike?' I replied, 'Yes, precisely similar, and similar will be your fate.' He endeavoured to answer my remarks, but it was manifest he was more troubled in spirit than I had ever seen him before.'

HARPER'S FERRY.
(FROM THE POTOMAC SIDE.)
Perhaps it will not be uninteresting to the reader, to vary a little the monotony of description which is entailed upon us by the character of the work, and give some account of the varieties of sporting on the Potomac.

This noble river abounds in fish, of which the principal are the white shad, the herring, and the sturgeon. The latter is taken in a way that, as far as we know, is entirely peculiar to this part of the country. The sturgeon is a noble denizen of the waters, weighing from seventy-five to one hundred and fifty pounds. His enormous leaps out of the water, and his alacrity at mounting a cascade, are accomplishments for which he is, as the advertisements phrase it, "favourably known." He has a habit, however, of scratching himself against any stationary object he finds in the river, which has been detected by the Potomac fishers, and employed, very successfully, to his detriment. A stout line, with a weight attached to it, is lowered from a boat, and a large hook, of peculiar contrivance, but without a bait, fastened to the extremity. The rubbing of the sturgeon against the line informs the fisherman of his neighbourhood, and, with a little skill, he succeeds in hooking him under the belly. The fish makes off with prodigious speed; the fisherman pays out line, and casts loose his painter; and away flies the boat with a speed and suddenness that seems like magic. A mile or so of this hard work is enough for the sturgeon, who gives out exhausted, and is easily drawn in. Some years ago, a negro, celebrated for his skill in this fishery, incautiously tied the line to his leg. The sudden jerk of the hooked fish pulled him overboard, and away he went down the stream, sometimes above, and sometimes under water, to the extreme astonishment of some people accidentally passing on the shore. He was an expert swimmer, however, and a heavy-limbed athletic fellow, and by remarkable coolness and courage he succeeded in bringing the sturgeon ashore. It is a singular fact, that this fish is only good in certain rivers: those of the Delaware, for example, being considered unfit to eat; and those of the rivers on either side of it, the Hudson and the Potomac, considered a great delicacy. It is recorded, by the way, that one of these enormous fish descended from an aerial leap into a ferry-boat, during the revolutionary war, and falling into the lap of an officer, seated on the gunwale, broke his thigh. Every passenger up this fine river has seen the sturgeon leaps; and an ascent of eight or ten feet above the water is not uncommon.

The shad and herring are taken by thousands, in nets, very much in the usual way.

The wild birds that frequent the bosom and shores of the Potomac, are very numerous. Among them are the swan, the wild goose, the red-head shoveler, the black-head shoveler, the duck and mallard, the black duck, the blue-winged teal, the green-winged teal, the widgeon, and, last not least, the far-celebrated canvass-back. This duck, which we believe is unrivalled in the world for richness of flavour, is one of a class called drift fowl, from their habit of floating in the middle of the river when at rest. The two species of shoveler have the same habit, and are scarcely inferior in flavour. The canvass-

42

back breeds, it is supposed, on the borders of the northern lakes, or on the shores of Hudson's Bay; and in their migrations confine their pasture almost exclusively to the Chesapeake and Potomac. They feed, it is well ascertained, on the bulbous root of a grass which grows on the flats in these rivers, and which is commonly known as wild celery. It is said, that during a hard winter, some forty years ago, a strong wind blew so much of the water off the flats of James river, that the remainder froze to the bottom, enclosing the long tops of this grass so closely in the ice, that when it broke up, and was floated off in the spring, it tore whole fields of it up by the roots, and destroyed the pasture. Since that time, the canvass-back has never been seen on the river.

The bald duck feeds very frequently among these water-fowl; and not having the power to dive entirely under water in search of food, he watches for the rising of the canvass-back, and, by his superior quickness on the wing, seizes on the celery the moment it appears above the surface, and escapes with it to the shore.

The canvass-back is often shot from behind blinds of brush, which conceal the sportsman, in the midst of their feeding ground. There is a practice, however, of tolling them in, as it is called, by shaking a coloured handkerchief tied to the branch of a decayed tree. On what propensity of the bird the success of this manœuvre is founded, it would be difficult to say. There is no doubt of the fact, however, that they are thus decoyed within gun-shot; and it is related of an old sportsman on the Potomac, that a long queue of red hair, which he wore in a brush, and shook over his shoulder, served the purpose admirably well. Perhaps we have yet to discover that birds have curiosity.

Among the many varieties of wild fowl found on the Potomac, below Harper's Ferry, is the wild swan. The young bird is considered a great delicacy; while the old one is hard and without flavour. In a book on the District of Columbia, by Mr. Elliott, there are some curious particulars respecting their habits, and the manner of taking them.

"This noble bird," says the author, "is seen floating near the shores, in flocks of some two or three hundred, white as the driven snow, and from time to time emitting fine sonorous, and occasionally melodious songs; so loud, that they might be heard, on a still evening, two or three miles. There are two kinds, so called from their respective notes— the one the trumpeter, and the other the hooper; the trumpeter is the largest, and when at full size will measure from five to six feet from the bill to the point of the toe, and from seven to eight feet from the tip of one wing to the tip of the other, when stretched and expanded. They are sagacious and wary, and depend more on the sight than on the sense of smell. On a neck nearly three feet in length, they are enabled to elevate their heads so as to see and distinguish, with a quick and penetrating eye, objects at a great distance; and by means of this same length of neck they feed in slack tides, by immersing, as is their habit, nearly all of the body, and throwing only their feet and tails out in three or four feet water, and on the flatty shores they frequent, generally beyond gun-shot; the sportsman availing himself, however, of a peculiar propensity (of which we shall presently speak more particularly) prevailing with them, and some of the other water fowl, often toll them within reach of their fire. The swans remain here the whole winter, only shifting their ground in severe weather, from the frozen to the open part of the river, and dropping down into the salts, where it is rarely frozen. They get into good condition soon after their arrival in autumn, and remain fat until toward spring, when, a few weeks before their departure (about the first of March), they gradually become thinner in flesh; and in the latter part of their sojourn here, are found so poor and light, that when shot the gunner gets nothing fit for use but the feathers. Whether this circumstance be owing to their having exhausted the means of subsistence at their feeding-places, or that they are taught by Him who rules the universe, in small as well as great things, thus by abstaining, to

43

prepare themselves for the long aerial voyages they are about to undertake, we pretend not to determine with certainty; there is nothing more wonderful in this, than in the fact, which is notorious, that they, by exercise, regularly and assiduously fit themselves for this continuous effort, to bear themselves through the air to the distance of perhaps a thousand miles or leagues. Large flocks are seen every day rising from the river, and taking a high position, flying out of sight, and apparently moving in a circuit to a considerable distance, again returning to or near the same place, during the last two or three weeks of their stay.

"The swan is tolled by a dog, that is taught to play about within easy call of his master, at the edge of the water; the hunter contrives to place himself behind a log, or some other cover well concealed, before he begins his operations, taking care to observe that the direction of the wind is not unfavourable to him, and that the flock he means to toll is near enough to distinguish such objects on the shore, and under no alarm at the time. By what motive these fowls are influenced, we have not heard satisfactorily explained; but certain it is, they are very commonly brought in from some hundreds of yards' distance, in this way, to within point-blank shot. It is said, and perhaps truly, in the case of the dog, that they fancy themselves in pursuit of some animal, as the fag, or mink, by which their young are annoyed at their breeding-places.

"The wild goose is yet more wary and vigilant to keep out of harm's way than the swan. He too is sharp-sighted, but depends much on his sense of smell for protection: this is so well known to the huntsman, that he never attempts, however he may be concealed from this bird, to approach it from the direction of the wind; since he would assuredly be scented before he could get within gun-shot, and left to lament his error, by the sudden flight of the whole flock. These geese, towards spring, often alight on the land, and feed on the herbage in fields; and sometimes in such numbers as to do great injury to the wheat fields on the borders of the river. When so employed they are difficult of approach, always taking a position at a distance from cover of any kind, and marching in a single and extended rank, flanked by a watch goose at each extremity; which, while all the others are busily feeding, and advancing with their heads down among the herbage, moves erect, keeping pace with his comrades,—his eyes and nose in a position so as to give him the earliest intelligence of the presence of an enemy, though at a great distance; and the moment such is perceived, it is communicated to the whole company by certain tones used for alarm; and immediately is responded to by a halt, and the lifting of heads; and an instant flight, or a deliberate return to feeding, takes place, according as the nature of the danger, after the examination, may be considered."

CALDWELL, LAKE GEORGE.
In the future poetry of America, Lake George will hold the place of Loch Katrine in Scotland. The best idea that can be given of it, indeed, to a person who has seen Loch Katrine, is to say, that it is the Trosachs on a little larger scale. There is the same remarkably clear water in both,—the same jutting and bold shores, small green islands, and bright vegetation; and the same profusion of nooks and bays. It struck me at Loch Katrine, that the waters seemed to have overflowed the dells of an undulating country, and left nothing visible but the small green hill-tops loaded with vegetation. The impression was owing, no doubt, to the reach of the shrubs and grass to the very edge of the water; and the same thing produces the same effect at Lake George. When the bosom of the lake is tranquil, the small islands, with their reflections below, look like globes of heaped-up leaves suspended in the air.

The extraordinary purity of the waters of Lake George procured for it the name of Lake Sacrament; and every stranger is struck with their singular transparency. It is singular, that the waters on every side of it,—those of Lake Champlain, for example, of the Hudson, and of the whole region between the Green Mountains and the Mississippi,—are more or less impregnated with lime, while Lake George alone is pellucid and pure. It receives its waters, probably, from subjacent springs.

The surface of this lake is said to be one hundred feet higher than Lake Champlain. Another, and probably a more correct estimate, makes the difference three hundred. There are three steps to the falls, which form the outlet into the latter lake; and the lower one, when the snow is melting in spring, is a cataract of uncommon beauty. Lake George is frozen over from three to four months; and it is remarked of it, that the ice does not sink, as in Lake Champlain, but gradually dissolves.

Before it became a part of the fashionable tour, this lake was a solitude, appropriated more particularly by the deer and the eagle. Both have nearly disappeared. The echo of the steam-boat, that has now taken the place of the noiseless canoe,—and the peppering of fancy sportsmen, that have followed the far-between but more effectual shots of the borderer's rifle,—have drawn from its shores these and other circumstances of romance. The only poetry of scene which can take the place of that of nature, is historical and legendary; and ages must lapse, and generations pass away, and many changes come over the land, before that time. We are in the interregnum, now, least favourable for poetry.

Caldwell is a flourishing town, built at the end of the lake, and remarkable for nothing, in itself, but a famous hotel, where scenery-hunters dine. We turn from this too succulent theme, to give an extract from the works of a grave and eminent divine; proving, by its glowing enthusiasm, the effect of this lovely scenery even on minds of the most serious bent.

"The whole scenery of this lake is greatly enhanced in beauty and splendour, by the progressive change which the traveller sailing on its bosom perpetually finds in his position, and by the unceasing variegations of light and shade which attend his progress. The gradual and the sudden openings of scoops and basins, of islands and points, of promontories and summits—the continual change of their forms, and their equally gradual and sudden disappearance,—impart to every object a brilliancy, life, and motion, scarcely inferior to that which is seen in the images formed by the camera-obscura, and in strength and distinctness greatly superior. Light and shade are here not only far more diversified, but are much more obvious, intense, and flowing, than in smooth, open countries. Every thing, whether on the land or water, was here affected by the changes of the day; and the eye, without forecast, found itself, however disposed on ordinary occasions to inattention, instinctively engaged, and fastened with emotions approximating to rapture. The shadows of the mountains, particularly on the west, floating slowly over the bosom of the lake, and then softly ascending that of the mountains on the east, presented to us, in a wide expanse, the uncommon and most pleasing image of one vast range of mountains slowly moving up the ascent of another.

"On the evening of Friday, the 1st of October, while we were returning from Ticonderoga, we were presented with a prospect superior to any which I ever beheld. An opening lay before us, between the mountains on the west and those on the east, gilded by the departing sunbeams. The lake, alternately glassy and gently rippled, of a light and exquisite sapphire, gay and brilliant with the tremulous lustre already mentioned floating upon its surface, stretched in prospect to a vast distance, through a great variety of larger and smaller apertures. In the chasm, formed by the mountains, lay a multitude of islands, differing in size, shape, and umbrage, and clothed in deeply-shaded green. Beyond them, and often partly hidden behind the tall and variously-figured trees with which they were tufted, rose, in the west and south-west, a long range of distant mountains, tinged with a deep misty azure, and crowned with an immense succession of lofty pines. Above the mountains, and above each other, were extended in great numbers long streaming clouds, of the happiest forms, and painted with red and orange light, in all their diversities of tincture.

"To complete the scenery of this lake, the efforts of cultivation are obviously wanting. The hand of the husbandman has already begun to clear these grounds, and will, at no great distance of time, adorn them with all the smiling scenes of agriculture. It does not demand the gift of prophecy to foresee, that the villas of opulence and refinement will, within half a century, add here all the elegances of art to the beauty and majesty of nature."

CENTRE HARBOUR, LAKE WINIPISEOGEE.

There are several considerable promontories which intrude into Lake Winipiseogee, and on one of them is built the town of Centre Harbour. The lake is near the middle of the state of New Hampshire, of a very irregular form, and at the western end is divided into three large bays. There are nine townships on its borders, of which Centre Harbour, the largest, is on the north-west side. The waters of the lake in some places are unfathomable, but abound with fish. It will still be some years, probably, before the navigation of this body of water will become of much importance.

Beside the beauty of nature, which is prodigal on the borders of this lovely lake, there is little of interest beyond what is found in the recollections of the Indian wars. Penhallow's History, which till lately has been a rare book, has rescued New Hampshire from the obscurity in which some of the other states remain, on these curious and interesting subjects. One wonders, in reading of the critical adventures of the early settlers, what offset the country could give them against such a frail tenure of life. "At one time," says the journal, "the people of Dunstable were advised of a party of two hundred and seventy Indians that were coming upon them. Their first descent was on the 3d of July, when they fell on a garrison that had twenty troopers in it, who, by their negligence, keeping no watch, suffered them to enter, which tended to the destruction of half their number. After that, a small party attacked Daniel Galusha's house, who held them in play for some time, till the old man's courage failed; when, on surrendering himself, he informed them of the state of the garrison; how that one man was killed, and only two men and a boy left; which caused them to rally anew, and with greater courage than before. Upon which, one with the boy got out on the back side, leaving only Jacob to fight the battle, who, for some time, defended himself with much bravery; but overpowered with force, and finding none to assist him, was obliged to quit it, and make his escape as well as he could: but before he got far, the enemy laid hold of him once and again; and yet, by much struggling, he rescued himself. Upon this, they burnt the house; and next day about forty more fell on Amesbury, where they killed eight: two, at the same time, who were at work in a field, hearing an outcry, hastened to their relief, but being pursued, ran to a deserted house, in which were two flankers, where each of them found an old gun, but neither of them fit for service; and if they were, had neither powder nor shot to load with: however, each took a flanker, and made the best appearance they could, by thrusting the muzzles of their guns outside the port-holes, crying aloud, 'Here they are, but do not fire till they come nearer;' which put the enemy into such a fright, that they instantly drew off."—Penhallow.

"From thence they went to Kingstown, where they killed and wounded several cattle. About the same time, Joseph English, who was a friend Indian, going from Dunstable to Chelmsford, with a man and his wife on horseback, was shot dead; the woman taken, but the man made his escape. On the 8th of July, five Indians, a little before night, fell on an out-house in Reading, where they surprised a woman with eight children: the former, with the three youngest, were instantly despatched, and the others they carried captive; but one of the children, unable to travel, they knocked on the head, and left in the swamp, concluding it was dead; but awhile after, it was found alive. The neighbourhood being alarmed, got ready by the morning, and coming on their track, pursued them so near that they recovered three of the children, and put the enemy in such a terror, that they not only quitted their plunder and blankets, but the other captive also: several strokes were afterwards made on Chelmsford, Sudbury, and Groton, where three soldiers, as they were going to public worship, were waylaid by a small party, who killed two, and made the other prisoner.

"At Exeter, a company of French Mohawks, who some time kept lurking about Captain Hilton's garrison, took a view of all that went in and out; and observing some to go with their scythes to mow, lay in ambush till they laid by their arms, and while at work, rushed on at once, and by intercepting them from their arms, killed four, wounded one, and carried three captive; so that out of ten, two only escaped. A while after, two of those that were taken, viz. Mr. Edward Hall and Samuel Myals, made their escape; but the fatigue and difficulty that they went through (besides the terror and fear they were under of being taken) were almost incredible; for in three weeks together, they had nothing to subsist on except a few lily roots, and the rinds of trees.

"It would be an endless task to enumerate the various sufferings that many groaned under, by long marching with heavy burdens through heat and cold; and when ready to faint for want of food, they were frequently knocked on the head: teeming women, in cold blood, have been ript open; others fastened to stakes and burnt alive; and yet the finger of God did eminently appear in several instances, of which I shall mention the following:—

"Of Rebekah Taylor, who after her return from captivity, gave me the following account:—That when she was going to Canada, on the back of Montreal river, she was violently insulted by Sampson, her bloody master, who without any provocation was resolved to hang her; and for want of a rope, made use of his girdle, which when he had fastened about her neck, he attempted to hoist her up on the limb of a tree (that hung in the nature of a gibbet), but in hoisting her, the weight of her body broke it asunder; which so exasperated the cruel tyrant that he made a second attempt, resolving if he failed in that, to knock her on the head; but before he had power to effect it, Bomaseen came along, and seeing the tragedy on foot, prevented the fatal stroke."

YALE COLLEGE AT NEWHAVEN.

Yale College was founded in the year 1700, sixty-five years after the erection of the first house in the Colony of Connecticut. Ten of the principal ministers, nominated by general consent of the clergy, met at New Haven, and formed themselves into a society, the object of which was to found a college in the colony. At their next meeting each brought a number of books, and presented them for the library, and the following year the Legislature granted them a charter, constituting them "Trustees of a Collegiate School in his Majesty's Colony of Connecticut."

The principal benefactor of the infant institution was the Hon. Elihu Yale, of London, Governor of the East India Company. This gentleman was descended from a family in Wales, which for many generations held the manor of Plas Grannow, near Rexon. His father, Thomas Yale, Esq., came from England with the first colonists of New Haven. In this town, Elihu, the subsequent benefactor of the College, was born, and at ten years of age he was sent to England. Thence he went to Hindostan, and after twenty years' residence, was made Governor of Madras. He returned to London with an immense fortune, was chosen Governor of the East India Company, and died at Rexon in 1721. "This gentleman," says the College historian, "sent, in several donations, to the Collegiate School, five hundred pounds sterling; and a little before his death, ordered goods to be sent out to the value of five hundred pounds more; but they were never received. In gratitude for this munificence, the Trustees, by a solemn act, named their seminary Yale College; a name which, it is believed, will convey the memory of his good works to distant generations."

Among other benefactors to this institution was the Rev. Dr. Berkeley, Dean of Derry, in Ireland, and afterwards Bishop of Cloyne. This distinguished divine came to America in 1732, for the purpose of establishing a college in the island of Bermuda; a purpose to which he sacrificed considerable time, property and labour. He had been promised twenty thousand pounds by the ministry for the completion of this work, but the sum was never paid, and the project failed. Dr. Berkeley then bought a farm in Newport, Rhode Island, and while residing there, became acquainted with the circumstances of Yale College, and ultimately made the institution a present of his farm, and sent the Trustees from England "the finest collection of books that ever came at one time to America."

Since this period Yale College has continued to thrive in means and usefulness, and it is now, in the numbers of its students, and in its practical advantages, we believe, the first College in the United States. That of Harvard, (founded sixty or seventy years earlier,) is better endowed, but more expensive and less frequented. It is a curious fact, in the early history of nations, by the way, that the Act to incorporate Harvard College was passed, and the College in operation, ten years after the first settlement of the Colony.

The whole amount of fees of tuition at Yale College is about thirty-five dollars a year, near seven pounds sterling. Board and every expense included, it is thought in New England that three hundred dollars (60l.) a year is a sufficient allowance for the education of a boy at this institution. The course of study embraces four years, and the discipline is impartial and severe. Instances occur annually of degrees refused, and degradations of standing in consequence of failures in examination; and over the morals of the students, particularly, the vigilance of the faculty is untiring and effective.

Perhaps one of the best, and certainly one of the peculiar advantages of Yale College, is the extent and excellence of the society in New Haven, and its accessibility to the students. The town contains near ten thousand inhabitants, most of them people of education, connected in some way with the College; or opulent families drawn thither by the extreme beauty of the town, and its air of refinement and repose. The upper classes of students mingle freely in this simple and pure society, which, it is not too much to say, is one of the most elegant and highly cultivated in the world. Polished manners and the usages of social life are thus insensibly gained with improvement of mind; and in a country like this, where those advantages are not attainable by all in early life, the privilege is inestimable.

The college buildings of New Haven are more remarkable for their utility than for the beauty of their architecture; but, buried in trees, and standing on the ridge of a sloping green, they have altogether a beautiful effect, and an air of elegant and studious repose.

Few strangers ever pass through New Haven without expressing a wish to take up their abode, and pass their days, among its picturesque avenues and gardens.

THE WILLEY-HOUSE—WHITE MOUNTAINS.

The particulars of what is called the Willey Tragedy are well known to all readers of newspapers. This family lived in the Notch of the White Mountains, under the western range, and consisted of nine persons. They had retired at night, when a very unusual noise in the mountains roused them from their beds, and, in terror at its increasing thunders, they unfortunately abandoned the house, and sought refuge in flight. A vast mass of earth and rocks, disengaged from the precipices above them, suddenly rushed down the side of the mountain, and sweeping every thing before it, divided in the rear of the house, reunited again, leaving it unharmed, and thundered down to the valley, overwhelming the fugitive family in its career. The manuscript journal of a friend, who had made two excursions to the spot, gives us an account of its present aspect.

"In a short time we came to the well-known house of the Willey family, which of course we paused to examine. Nothing can be conceived more lonely than this wild place. The mountains tower on both sides of the valley to the height of four or five hundred feet, with deep channels worn into their sides by the winter torrents; and in many places the rocks are left bare for acres by the slides of avalanches that have rushed into the valley. The house in which the unfortunate family dwelt stands under the western range of mountains, and the avalanche came down nearly from the summit. We remained gazing on the scene for some time. The sky above was clear, and spanned the interval between the mountains, seeming to rest on their summits, while a swift breeze drove over the hills below, in swift succession, a few thin and fleecy clouds. The wind entered the outer door of the desolate dwelling, which had been left open, with a broken chair set against it; and as it surged back and forth, violently shut and opened the inner doors, with a noise that seemed the voice of the very spirit of desolation. The effect was startling and dismal."

This is, we believe, the most disastrous avalanche on record in this country, and the only one of any importance, which was merely a descent of earth and rocks. What is called a cloud-burst is not uncommon in the mountainous regions of the north; and there are several striking examples recorded.

In the autumn of 1784, in the latter part of the night, a deluge of water descended from Saddle Mountain, in Massachusetts. A family, which lived in a house at some distance from the foot of the mountain, not far from a brook, were suddenly awakened out of their sleep by the united roaring of the wind and the torrent. In their flight they hastily dressed themselves, and escaped from the house, the ground-floor of which was by this time six inches under water. When they returned in the morning, they found the house so completely swept away, that no part of it was left. The brook, through the channel of which this flood discharged itself, had never before, even in the highest freshets, approached the house by a considerable distance.

Subsequent examination of the mountain disclosed that the descent of water commenced not far from the summit; for two or three rods above the spot where the ground first began to be broken, the trees and shrubs appear to have been swept away by the violence of the deluge. The broken ground is, at first, not more than six feet wide, but rapidly becomes wider as it descends; so that within one hundred and fifty feet it is about three rods in breadth, and in the widest place five or six. Towards the lower limit its breadth gradually diminishes, until it terminates in a gutter, which in some places is five or six feet deep; this continues several rods, and then branches into other channels, which, though covered with leaves and moss, are discernible quite down to the brook at the foot of the mountain. The whole length of the broken ground is about one hundred and thirty rods. Towards the bottom there were standing the stumps of large trees, whose tops were broken off by the deluge; and above they were entirely swept away, not leaving a trace. By what means a mass of water, sufficient for these phenomena, is collected and suspended over the mountains, or what occasioned the disruption of the mass of earth and rock which overwhelmed the family in the White Mountains, are points not easily settled.

BATTLE MONUMENT, BALTIMORE.

This monument stands on the summit of a rising ground, in the centre of one of the best built squares of Baltimore, and is a very considerable ornament to the town. It is intended to commemorate the name and fame of those citizens of Baltimore who fell in its defence in 1814. An Egyptian base, raised to the height of about four feet from the pavement of the street, is surmounted by a column, representing fasces, upon the bands of which are placed in bronze letters the names of the thirty-nine citizens. On each angle of the base are griffins, and the lower part of the column is ornamented with bassi relievi, representing scenes of the contest. The whole is crowned by a statue personifying the city, with the eagle at her side, holding a laurel wreath. The entire height of the monument is fifty-two feet.

The defence of Baltimore was one of the most spirited of the many gallant actions on our sea-board and frontier during the late war; and it occurred more opportunely, as it followed so closely upon the defeat at Bladensburgh, which, though inevitable from the superior numbers of the enemy, was still accompanied with the mortification inseparable from such disaster.

After the embarkation of the troops under General Ross, (who had bought his victory at Bladensburgh with the loss of nearly a thousand men,) Admiral Cochrane concentrated his fleet, and made preparations for the attack on Baltimore. The whole squadron, amounting to forty vessels, sailed soon after for the Patapsco, and arriving near North Point, twelve miles from the city, the ships of the line anchored across the channel, and commenced the debarkation of troops. By the morning of the 12th of September about 8,000 soldiers, sailors, and marines, were in readiness to march upon the town, and sixteen bomb vessels and frigates proceeded up the river, and anchored within two miles and a half of Fort McHenry.

This garrison, which was mainly relied on for the protection of the city, was defended by about 5,000 men, and a detachment of about 3,000 was sent on by the North Point road to annoy or engage the enemy at his approach. Intelligence soon came in, that a light corps was advancing; and two companies of infantry, with a few riflemen, and ten artillerists with a single four-pounder, proceeded half a mile, and met and engaged the main body. The situation of the ground would not admit of the cooperation of the artillery and cavalry; and the infantry and riflemen sustained the whole action with great gallantry. The advance of the enemy was checked, and Major-General Ross and several other British officers killed.

The detachment now fell back upon the main line of the American force, and after some skirmishing with rockets and artillery at a distance, the whole force of the enemy pushed forward, and attacked the two regiments on the left with great impetuosity. These being thrown into confusion, a general fire was opened upon the British line, and a vigorous action followed, which lasted till four o'clock. At that hour the American force amounting to but about 1,400, and the British to about 7,000, General Stucker fell back upon the reserve regiment, and was joined by some other companies, who took position with him within half a mile of the entrenchments.

Early the following morning the Admiral made signals to the British officer in command on shore, that the frigates, bomb-ships, and flotilla of barges, would take their stations to bombard the town and fort in the course of the morning. The land forces accordingly moved forward, and took up a position two miles eastward of the entrenchments. The day was chiefly passed in manœuvring; but Colonel Brooke, after a vain attempt to make a detour through the country, concentrated the English force directly in front of the American line, drove in the outposts, and made preparations for an attack in the night.

The night was stormy; and in the morning it was discovered that the enemy had abandoned his position. The troops were re-embarked, and a bombardment commenced, which lasted till the following morning, during which a fleet of barges attempted to storm Fort Covington, but were repulsed with great loss. With the failure of this attempt the undertaking was abandoned altogether, and the fleet stood down the river.

When the bombardment commenced, the fort opened its batteries upon the ships; but, the shot falling short, the little garrison were compelled to keep their post without retaliation. There were four killed and twenty-four wounded in the entrenchments, and among the former were two very gallant young men, Lieutenants Clagett and Clem, volunteer officers.

The entire loss of the British could not be ascertained. That of the Americans on the field was about 150, which, added to those in the fort, makes a total of 178.

A FOREST, ON LAKE ONTARIO.

The view over this immense forest was taken in the Tuscarora reservation, from an Indian cabin, which serves as a sort of halting-place for travellers to Niagara. We arrived here about noon, emerging from a tract of deep woods which had darkened the road for several miles, and glancing off to the right, discovered that we were following a high ridge, from which extended, with a radius of forty miles, one unbroken sea of foliage. A thin silver line on the very rim of the horizon looked brighter than the sky, and we found on inquiry that it was Lake Ontario, which, with its thread of bright light, forms a limit to what, else, were an object as boundless as the sea.

An Indian woman of about forty, dressed very neatly, came out to offer for sale specimens of Indian workmanship, such as moccasins, pouches, &c.; and, among other things, a beautiful little model of a bark canoe. De Kalm, who travelled in this country in 1749, gives a very detailed account of the making of a canoe. He was going to Canada under the escort of a party of Indians, who, on coming to a portage of forty miles, between the Hudson and Lake Champlain, (now superseded by a canal,) were compelled to leave their canoe and build another.

"The making of the canoe," he says, "took up half yesterday and all this day. To make such a boat, they pick out a thick, tall elm, with a smooth bark, and with as few branches as possible. This tree is cut down, and great care is taken to prevent the bark from being hurt by falling against other trees, or against the ground. With this view some do not fell the trees, but climb to the top of them, split the bark, and strip it off; which was the method our boat-builder took. The bark is split on one side, in a straight line along the tree, as long as the boat is intended to be; at the same time the bark is carefully cut from the stem a little way on both sides of the slit, that it may more easily separate. The bark is then peeled off very carefully, and particular care is taken not to make any holes in it; this is easy when the sap is in the trees; and at other seasons the tree is heated by the fire for that purpose.

51

"The bark thus stripped off is spread on the ground, in a smooth place, turning the inside downwards, and the rough outside upwards; and to stretch it better, some logs of wood or stones are carefully put on it, which press it down. Then the sides of the bark are gently bent upwards, in order to form the sides of the boat. Some sticks are then fixed into the ground at the distance of three or four feet from each other, in the curve line in which the sides of the boat are intended to be, supporting the bark intended for the sides. The sides of the bark are then bent in the form which the boat is to have, and according to that, the sticks are either put near or further off.

"The ribs of the canoe are made of thick branches of hickory, they being tough and pliable. They are cut into several flat pieces, about an inch thick, and bent into the form which the ribs require, according to their places in the broader or narrower part of the boat. The upper edge on each side is made of two thin poles, of the length of the boat, which are put close together on the side, being flat where they are joined. The edge of the bark is put between these two poles, and sewed up with threads of the mouse-wood, or other tough bark, or with roots.

"After this is done, the poles are sewed together, and being bent properly, both ends join at each end of the boat, where they are tied together with ropes. To prevent the widening of the boat at the top, three or four transverse bands are put across it, from one edge to the other, at the distance of thirty or forty inches from each other, made of hickory.

"As the bark at the two ends of the boat cannot be put so close together as to keep out the water, the crevices are stopped up with the crushed or pounded bark of the red elm, which in that state looks like oakum. Some pieces of bark are put on the ribs of the boat, without which the foot would easily pierce the thin and weak bottom. The side of the bark which runs next the wood thus becomes the outside of the boat, because it is smooth and slippery, and cuts the water with less difficulty than the other.

"The building of these boats is not always quick; for sometimes it happens that after peeling the bark off an elm, and carefully examining it, it is found pierced with holes and slits, or is too thin to venture one's life in. That which we made was big enough to bear four persons, with our baggage, which weighed somewhat more than a man.

"All possible precautions must be taken in rowing on rivers with bark canoes; for when rowing fast, a broken branch under water would carry half the boat away. To get into it also requires great care, for the heels may very easily pierce through the bottom."

VIADUCT ON THE BALTIMORE AND WASHINGTON RAIL-ROAD.

The Patuxent, which is leaped over so lightly at this place by the arches of the Viaduct, becomes, ere long, a stream which is not only respectable in size, but most respectable in story. It will ever be associated with the name and fame of the gallant Barney, who, though his exertions could not prevent ultimate defeat, did much to sustain his country's honour, and has made his own imperishable.

While the British squadron was blockading the eastern coast during the summer of 1814, Commodore Barney sailed from Baltimore in command of a flotilla consisting of a cutter, two gun-boats, a galley, and nine large barges, for the protection of the inlets and harbours in the several parts of the bay. On the 1st of June, being at the mouth of the Patuxent, he discovered two schooners, one of which carried eighteen guns; and immediately gave chase. The schooners were joined, however, by a large ship, which despatched a number of barges to their assistance; and the commodore sailed up the Patuxent to avoid being cut off from the Potomac. The schooners and barges following him, he engaged and drove them back, and then anchored within three miles of the seventy-four. In the course of a few days, the enemy was reinforced by a rasee and a sloop of war; and joining the barges of these vessels, they followed the flotilla into St. Leonard's Creek, across which Commodore Barney formed his boats in line of battle. A sharp engagement ensued, the enemy gave way, and the flotilla pursued them to within a short distance of their shipping. In the afternoon, the enemy made another attempt with twenty barges and two schooners. After a warm action, the barges were driven back upon the eighteen-gun schooner, which, in attempting to beat out, was so severely handled, that her crew ran her aground and abandoned her. On the 26th, a corps of artillery arrived from Washington to the commodore's assistance, and a combined attack was made on the whole squadron. The action continued two hours; at the end of which the enemy's ships were driven from their anchorage, and stood down the river.

The cessation of hostilities in Europe, enabled the British government to send out powerful reinforcements to their fleets and armies in America; and Sir Alexander Cochrane soon arrived with thirty sail, having on board several thousand men, under command of Major General Ross. This force entered the Chesapeake, and a plan of attack on Washington, Alexandria, and Baltimore, was adopted. Admiral Cochrane very honourably informed the Secretary of State that he had orders to lay waste all the accessible towns on the coast; and the fleet, in two divisions, soon after approached the capital by the Potomac and the Patuxent.

In obedience to orders, Commodore Barney blew up his flotilla in the Patuxent, and with his seamen and marines, joined the army under General Winder. General Ross landed six thousand men at the head of frigate navigation, and, with five thousand, General Winder met him at Bladensburg. The action commenced at mid-day. Commodore Barney had been placed with his battery in the main road by which the enemy advanced; and after two or three vain attempts were made to pass him, the main column fell back in disorder, and it was found necessary to flank his right. The British were gaining ground, however, in every other part of the line; and Commodore Barney was soon left with his small force standing alone.

General Ross had now nearly complete command of the field; the ammunition waggons had been driven off in the disorder, and the commodore was reduced to a single round of cartridge. He had besides received a severe wound in the thigh. Thus situated, he gave reluctant orders for retreat; and after being carried a short distance, he fell, exhausted with loss of blood. He was soon after taken prisoner, and removed to the enemy's hospital, where he was treated, by the orders of General Ross, with the greatest kindness; and, on his recovery, released on his parole.

After his victory at Bladensburgh, General Ross marched directly to the capital, and proceeded immediately to burn all the public buildings, library, &c. Then, as now, Washington was merely a diplomatic capital, very thinly populated; and the few inhabitants were unable to make any show of resistance. No comment is necessary on an act which the English nation itself was the first to condemn.

The division of the enemy's fleet which sailed up the Potomac, consisting of eight sail, was directed to attack Alexandria. That small town surrendered, and obtained a stipulation, upon very ungenerous conditions, that their houses should not be entered or destroyed. Captain Gordon, who was in command, sailed soon after down the river with a fleet of prize vessels taken from the town, and a great amount of property. He received some damage from the batteries lower down, but joined the rest of the squadron in the Chesapeake, and accompanied them in their less successful attacks on Baltimore.

We think the "City of Monuments," as the last-mentioned town is called, should erect a monument to the memory of Barney.

"A TRIBUTE TO THE BRAVE.

"Though furled be the banner of blood on the plain,
And rusted the sabre once crimsoned with gore;
Though hushed be the ravens that croaked o'er the slain,
And calmed into silence the battle's loud roar;
Though Peace with her rosy smile gladden the vales,
And Commerce unshackled dance over the wave;
Though Music and Song may enliven the gales,
And Joy crown with roses and myrtle the brave;
Like spirits that start from the sleep of the dead,
Our heroes shall rouse when the 'larum shall blow;
Then Freedom's broad flag on the wind shall be spread,
And Valour's sword flash in the face of the foe.
Our Eagle shall rise 'mid the whirlwinds of war,
And dart through the dun cloud of battle his eye—
Shall spread his wide wings on the tempest afar,
O'er spirits of valour that conquer or die.
And ne'er shall the rage of the conflict be o'er,
And ne'er shall the warm blood of life cease to flow,
And still 'mid the smoke of the battle shall roam
Our Eagle—till scattered and fled be the foe.
When Peace shall disarm War's dark brow of its frown,
And roses shall bloom on the soldier's rude grave—
Then Honour shall weave of the laurel a crown,
That Beauty shall bind on the brow of the brave."—Percival.

INDIAN FALLS,
OPPOSITE WEST POINT.

This is a secluded and delicious bit of nature, hidden amid rocks and woods, on the shore of the Hudson, but possessing a refinement and an elegance in its wildness which would almost give one the idea that it was an object of beauty in some royal park. One of the most secret streams that feed this finest of our rivers, finds its way down through a winding and almost trackless channel; and after fretting over rocks, and loitering in dark and limpid pools for several miles, suddenly bursts out over a precipice of fifty feet, and fills with its clear waters the sheltered basin seen in the drawing. Immense trees overhang it on every side, and follow the stream still on in its course; and, in the depth of summer, the foaming current scarcely catches a ray of the sun from its source to its outlet. The floor of the basin below the Falls is pebbly, the water is clear and cool, the spot secluded, and, in all respects, Nature has formed it for a bath. A fair and famous lady, residing a summer or two since at West Point, was its first known Musidora, and the limpid and bright basin is already called after her name.

A large party visiting at a hospitable house, where the artist and his travelling companion were entertained during the heat of the last summer, proposed to accompany him on his visit to the Indian Falls. Excursions on the banks of the Hudson are usually made in boats; but it was necessary to see some points of view from the hills between, and we walked out to the stables to see what could be done for vehicles and cattle. A farm waggon, with its tail up in the air, built after an old Dutch fashion, which still prevails in New York,—a sort of loosely jointed, long, lumbering vehicle, which was meant to go

54

over any rock smaller than a beer-barrel without upsetting—was the only "consarn," as the "help" called it, which would hold the party. With straw in the bottom, and straps put across from peg to peg, it would carry eleven, and the driver.

Horses were the next consideration; and here we were rather staggered. A vicious old mare, that kept a wheelwright and a surgeon in constant employ,—and a powerful young colt, half broken,—were the only steeds in stable. However either might be made to go alone, they had never been tried together; and the double waggon harness was the worse for service. The "help" suggested very sensibly that the load would be too heavy to run away with, and that if the mare kicked, or the colt bolted—or, in short, if any thing happened, except backing over a precipice, we had only to sit still and let them do their "darndest."

We cobbled the harness in its weak spots, shook down the straw for the ladies, nailed up the tail-board, which had lost its rods, got the cattle in, and brought up quietly to the door. The ladies and the champagne were put in, and the colt was led off by the bit, shaking his head, and catching up his hind leg; while the demure old mare drew off tamely and steadily, "never wicked," as the ploughman said, "till you got her dander up with a tough hill." The driver had a chain with a list bottom, and, having had some practice in Charing Cross and Fleet Street, fingered his reins and flourished his maple whip through the village, evidently not thinking himself or his driving de la petite bière.

The road, which followed the ridges of the superb hills skirting the river opposite West Point, was, in some places, scarce fit even for a bridle-path; and, at every few paces, came a rock, which we believed passable when we had surged over it—not before. The two ill-matched animals drew to a wonder; and the ladies and the champagne had escaped all damage, till, as the enemy of mankind would have it, our ambitious whip saw stretching out before him a fair quarter of a mile of more even road. A slight touch of the whip sent off the colt in a jump, carrying away the off trace with the first spring; the old mare struck into a gallop, and, with the broken trace striking against the colt's heels, and the whippletree parallel with the pole, away they went as nearly in a tandem as the remaining part of the harness would allow. The tail-board soon flew off, and let out two unsuspecting gentlemen, who had placed their backs and their reliance upon it; and the screams of the ladies added what was wanting to raise the "dander" of the old mare to its most unpleasant climax. The straps gave way, the ladies rolled together in the straw, the driver tossed about on his list-bottomed chain, the champagne corks flew,—and presently, as if we were driven by a battering-ram against a wall, we brought up with a tremendous crash, and stood still. We had come to a sharp turn in the road; and the horses, unable to turn, had leaped a low stone wall, and breaking clear of every thing, left us on one side, while they thrashed the ripe wheat with the whippletrees on the other.

The ladies were undamaged, fortunately; and, with one champagne bottle saved from the wreck, we completed the excursion to the Falls on foot, and were too happy to return by water.

COLUMBIA BRIDGE, OVER THE SUSQUEHANNA.
This fine bridge is a mile and a half in length, and forms a beautiful span over the broad waters of the river at this place. The many windings of the Susquehanna make its shallowness and incapacity for navigation less a disadvantage than would have been felt on a more direct water-course; and the ingenuity and enterprise of the country in the construction of canals, bridges, and rail-roads, have left nothing to desire in the matter of facilities for travel. It is always a reasonable query to any, except a business traveller, whether the saving of time and fatigue in the wonderful improvements in locomotion is

an equivalent for the loss of rough adventure and knowledge of the detail of a country acquired by hardship and delay. Contrast the journey over a rail-road at a pace of fifteen miles in the hour, through the rough, the picturesque valley of the Susquehanna, with a journey over the same ground ninety years ago, as presented in the travels of Peter Kalm. He was on horseback, with Indian guides.

"About sunset it cleared up, and we encamped on the east branch of the Susquehanna. In the night it thundered and rained very fast, and took us at a disadvantage; for we had made no shelter to keep off the rain, neither could we see it till just over our heads, and it began to fall.

"One of our Indians cut four sticks, five feet long, and stuck both ends in the ground, at two feet distance one from another; over these he spread his watch-coat, and crept through them, and then fell to singing. In the mean time, we were setting poles slantwise in the ground, tying others across them; over which we spread our blanket, and crept close under it, with a fire before us, and fell fast asleep. I waked a little after midnight and found our fire almost out; so I got the hatchet and felled a few saplings, which I laid on, and made a rousing fire, though it rained stoutly; and lying down once more, I slept sound all night.

"In the morning, when we had dried our blankets, we kept along the side of a hill, and looked about us, not having had such an opportunity for two days, on account of the forest. The valley differed from all I had ever seen before, in its easy and fruitful ascent and descent,—in its great width, everywhere crowned with noble and lofty woods,—but above all, in being entirely free from naked rocks and sharp precipices."

A night or two after, our traveller fell in with a variety of Indian character I never have seen noticed elsewhere:—

"Soon after we were laid down to sleep, and our fire almost burnt out, we were entertained by a comical fellow, disguised in as odd a dress as Indian folly could invent. He had on a clumsy vizard of wood, coloured black, with a nose four or five inches long, a grinning mouth set awry, and furnished with long teeth; round the eyes were circles of bright brass, surrounded by a larger circle of white paint. From his forehead hung long tresses of buffalo's hair; and from the catch part of his head (his tuft) hung ropes, made of the plaited husks of Indian corn.

"I cannot recollect the whole of his dress, but that it was equally uncouth. He carried in one hand a large staff, in the other a calabash, with small stones in it for a rattle; and this he rubbed up and down with his staff. He came in at the further end of the wigwam, and, holding up his head, made a noise like the braying of an ass. I asked Weisar, who, as well as myself, lay next the alley, what noise that was. Shickalamy, the chief, who thought I was scared, called out, 'Lie still, John!' I never heard him speak so much English before.

"The jack-pudding presently came up to us, and an Indian boy came with him and kindled our fire, that we might see his glittering eyes and antic postures, as he hobbled round the fire. Sometimes he would turn the buffalo's hair on one side, that we might take a better view of his ill-favoured phiz. When he had tired himself, (which was some time after he had well tired us,) the boy that attended him struck two or three smart blows on the floor, at which the hobgoblin seemed surprised; and, on repeating them, he jumped fairly out of doors and disappeared.

"I suppose this was to divert us, and get some tobacco; for, as he danced about, he would hold out his hand to receive this gratification, for which, as often as he received it, he would return an awkward compliment. After this farce, we endeavoured to compose

56

ourselves to sleep, but towards morning were again disturbed by a drunken squaw coming into the cabin, frequently complimenting us and singing."

We doubt if any traveller's journal on the Mauch Chunk rail-road can show as diverting a page. There are no incidents now-a-days short of a boiler bursting.

GENESSEE FALLS, ROCHESTER.

In the three thousand miles between the Atlantic and the Rocky Mountains, there may be said to be three water-steps formed by the different levels of Lake Ontario, Lake Erie, and Lake Superior. Niagara and the Genessee river fall over the middle step, the edge of which is formed by the brow of a bed of limestone, computed to be four hundred and ten feet above the level of Lake Ontario. Saint Lawrence may thus be said to take but three leaps from the Rocky Mountains to the ocean—an agility which, one would suppose, might have saved the holy martyr from his gridiron.

The ledge over which these two celebrated falls are precipitated, comes out of Canada from an immense distance, and keeps its course along the shore of Lake Ontario, in a direction nearly due east. At the Genessee Falls, as at Niagara, the descent to the lake is between the walls of a tremendous ravine, the grandeur of which seems to have had no terror for the souls of manufacturers. The thriving village of Rochester stands round the lip of the fall; and if you talk to the inhabitants of the beauty of the cascade, they stop your mouth, and strike calculation dumb, with the number of sledge-hammers, nail-cutters, mill-stones, and cotton-jennies, it carries; the product per diem; the corresponding increase of population, et cetera et cetera—the only instance in the known world of a cataract turned, without the loss of a drop, through the pockets of speculators.

The Genessee river rises in the Alleghany Mountains, and it is not for want of poetical names on its banks that it is not a poetical river. Its source is ten miles below Nunda, between the head waters of the Owago and the Cawanisque rivers; and it runs one hundred and fifty miles, receiving tribute from the Canassaraga and Angelica creeks, and the Canesus and Honcoye outlets. It has a great reputation for fertility; and along its valley lies the celebrated farm of Mr. Wadsworth, the agriculturist, who holds in this country the place occupied in England by Mr. Coke of Holkham—now Earl of Leicester.

The Rapids of the Genessee commence a mile above the Fall at Rochester, and descend, when there is much water, with great swiftness and beauty. The first pitch of the stream is ninety-seven perpendicular feet; after which it goes sullenly on down the ravine—black, where it is not covered with foam—till, forty rods below, it takes another leap of one hundred and six feet, at a place called Carthage. We suggested to the landlord that the fall at Carthage should be called after Marius, but he did not see the propriety of it very clearly.

The Genessee Fall, like Niagara, is gradually backing up. It is computed that the latter wears back a rood every three years—the former much less, of course. There is little doubt among the geologists, that the Genessee at one time ran directly into Lake Ontario without much of a cascade, but that, on the retreat of the lake, the surface of which has perceptibly lowered, the stream began to wear back with the attrition of the fall, and they are now three miles asunder. An aqueduct of the great Erie canal runs close across the head of the Fall at Rochester, and is built in full confidence that the cascade will continue the sobriety and order it has hitherto preserved in its retreat. If it were to take a long step up stream of a sudden, that great vein of the west would breathe more freely than is provided for by the "weirs and feeders." This aqueduct at Rochester is a work of some pretension. It is seven hundred and fifty feet in length, and has twelve piers and eleven arches, two of which are over Mill-races. A path is railed off on the side of the canal, and it forms a picturesque promenade across the bed of the river.

The country about the Falls of the Genessee was a wilderness in 1812. Now it contains nearly twenty thousand inhabitants, and is one of the most flourishing towns in the world. In 1830, it supported one daily, two semi-weekly, and three weekly newspapers; and in the single year of 1826, (an age ago, by the Rochester reckoning,) it exported two hundred and two thousand nine hundred barrels of flour. It seems to grow visibly before your eyes; the eternal hammering and clipping of bricks, and heaps of rubbish, remind the traveller so pertinaciously that it is in a state of transition only. The hotels are excellent, and the inhabitants famed for their public spirit, hospitality, and enterprise—the latter, of course.

VIEW OF THE FERRY AT BROOKLYN, NEW YORK

Brooklyn is as much a part of New York, for all purposes of residence and communication, as "the Borough" is of London. The steam ferry-boats cross the half-mile between it and the city every five minutes; and in less time than it usually takes to thread the press of vehicles on London Bridge, the elegant equipages of the wealthy cross to Long Island for the afternoon drive; morning visits are interchanged between the residents in both places—and, indeed, the east river is hardly more of a separation than the same distance in a street.

Brooklyn is the shire-town of King's County, and by this time, probably, is second in population only to New York. Land there, has risen in value to an enormous extent within the last few years; and it has become the fashion for business-men of New York to build and live on the fine and healthy heights above the river, where they are nearer their business, and much better situated than in the outskirts of the city itself. The town of Brooklyn is built on the summit and sides of an elevation springing directly from the bank of the river, and commanding some of the finest views in America. The prospect embraces a large part of East River, crowded with shipping, and tracked by an endless variety of steamers, flying through the channel in quick succession; of the city of New York, extending, as far as the eye can see, in closely piled masses of architecture; of the Hudson, and the shore of Jersey, beyond; of the bay and its bright islands, and of a considerable part of Long and Staten Islands, and the Highlands of Neversink. A more comprehensive, lively, and interesting view is nowhere to be found.

Historically, Brooklyn will long be remembered for the battle fought in its neighbourhood between the British and Hessians under the command of General Howe, and the Americans under the immediate command of Generals Putnam and Sullivan. It was a contest of a body of ill-disciplined militia against twice their number of regular troops, and ended in defeat; but the retreat conducted by General Washington saved the army, and relieved a little the dark fortunes of the day.

The American forces were composed of militia and raw recruits, and without even dragoons to serve as videts. They were stationed on a chain of eminences running from Yellow Hook towards Hempstead; and the British, from the Ferry between Staten and Long Islands, through the level country to the village of Flatland. From the last-mentioned place, a strong column, led by General Clinton and Lord Percy, marched into the Jamaica Road, through an unoccupied pass in this chain of hills on the right, and turned the left of the American army. General Grant at the same time attacked the right of the Americans under the command of Lord Sterling, posted near the Ferry; while the fleet commenced a powerful cannonade upon a battery at Red Hook, to draw off the attention of the Americans from the main attack directed by Sir Henry Clinton.

As soon as the Americans perceived that the enemy had gained the rear, they were thrown into confusion, and attacks were made on the centre, commanded by General Sullivan, and the right, commanded by Lord Stirling, and both divisions completely routed. A gallant attempt was made by the latter officer, which, though unavailing, facilitated the retreat of part of the troops under his command. He was himself taken prisoner, as were also Generals Sullivan and Woodhull. The number of Americans killed is estimated at four hundred, and the wounded and prisoners at a thousand.

General Washington, who had passed over from New York to Brooklyn during the heat of the action, perceived that nothing could be done to turn the fortune of the day, and that the only thing to be accomplished was a retreat. The British were only waiting for a wind to move their shipping into the East River, and the next morning might find the ferry in their possession. The British were encamped within six hundred yards of him; and the wind, until eleven o'clock, was unfavourable. At that hour it lulled, and a thick fog covered the bosom of the river. The army commenced their embarkation under this fortunate protection; and the whole of the forces, with their ammunition, provision, horses, waggons, &c. crossed undisturbed. The retreat was discovered by the British half an hour after the evacuation. The sound of their pickaxes was distinctly heard within the American lines during the embarkation.

VIEW OF THE RAIL-ROAD TO UTICA,
TAKEN AT LITTLE FALLS.

Before the completion of the Rail-road, when travellers to the West were contented with the philosophic pace of the canal-boat, one might take up a novel at Little Falls, and come fairly to the sequel by the time the steersman cried out "Bridge!" at Utica. There were fifteen miles between them in those days; but now (to a man of indistinct ideas of geography, at least, and a traveller on the Rail-road) they are as nearly run together as two drops on the window-pane. The intermediate distance is, by all the usual measurements of wear and time, annihilated.

All this is very pleasant to people in a hurry; and as most people in our busy country come under that category, it is a very pleasant thing for the white man altogether. There is a class of inhabitants of the long valley of the Mohawk, however, of whose sufferings, by the advance of the white man's enterprise, this is not the first, though it may be the least, and last. The poor half-naked Oneida, who ran by the side of the once crowded canal-boat for charity, has not time, while the rail-car passes, even to hold out his hand!

The Oneidas have not long been beggars by the road side. They were one of the five tribes confederated under the name of the Iroquois, who gloried in having fought their way into the country of the Mohawks, and kept their place and possessions in the midst of them; the latter tribe enjoying the undisputed honour of being an original people on the soil. Though merged in a confederacy, however, the Oneidas had their own chiefs; and a mythology of their own, which is not a little curious. It will not be mal-apropos, accompanying drawings of the towns that have usurped their ancient seat, to give some account of their ideas upon the origin of the earth and the human race.

According to the Oneida, an unlimited expanse of water once filled the space now occupied by the world which we inhabit. At this time the human family dwelt in a country situated in the upper regions of the air, abounding in every thing conducive to the comfort and pleasure of life. The inhabitants were strangers to death, and its harbingers, pain and disease; whilst their minds were free from the corroding passions of jealousy, hatred, and revenge.

At length, however, an event occurred which interrupted their tranquillity, and introduced care and anxiety, until then unknown. A certain youth was noticed to withdraw himself from the circle of their social amusements: the solitary recesses of the grove became his favourite walks. Care and chagrin were depicted in his countenance, and his body, from long abstinence, presented to the view of his friends the mere skeleton of a man. Anxious solicitude in vain explored the cause of his grief; until, at length, debilitated both in body and mind, he yielded to the importunity of his associates, and promised to disclose the cause of his trouble on condition that they would dig up by the roots a certain white pine-tree, lay him in his blanket by the margin of the hole, and seat his wife by his side. In a moment all hands were ready. The fatal tree was taken up by the roots; in doing which, the earth was perforated, and a passage opened into the abyss below. The blanket was spread by the hole, the youth laid upon it, and his wife, then in a state of pregnancy, took her seat by his side. The multitude, eager to learn the cause of such strange and unusual conduct, pressed around; when, on a sudden, to their horror and astonishment, he seized upon the woman, and precipitated her headlong into the regions of darkness below; then, rising from the ground, he informed the assembly, that he had for some time suspected the chastity of his wife, and that, having now disposed of the cause of his trouble, he should soon recover his usual health and vivacity.

All those amphibious animals which now inhabit this world then roamed through the watery waste to which the woman, in her fall, was hastening. The Loon first discovered her coming, and called a council in haste to prepare for her reception; observing, that the animal which approached was a human being, and that earth was indispensably necessary for its accommodation. The first subject of deliberation was, who should support the burden.

The sea-bear first presented himself for a trial of his strength. Instantly the other animals gathered round and scrambled on his back; while the bear, unable to support the weight, sank beneath the surface of the water, and was, by the whole assembly, judged unequal to the task of supporting the earth. Several others in succession presented themselves as candidates for the honour, with similar success. Last of all the turtle modestly advanced, tendering his broad shell as the basis of the earth now about to be formed. The beasts then made a trial of his strength to bear, heaping themselves on his back; and finding their united pressure unable to sink him below the surface, adjudged to him the honour of supporting the world.

A foundation being thus provided, the next subject of deliberation was, how to procure earth. Several of the most expert divers plunged to the bottom of the sea, and came up dead; but the mink, at last, though he shared the fate of the others, brought up in his claws a small quantity of earth. This was placed on the back of the turtle.

In the mean time, the woman continued falling, and, at length, alighted on the turtle's back. The earth had already grown to the size of a man's foot, where she stood, with one foot covering the other. Shortly, she had room for both feet, and was soon able to sit down. The earth continued to expand; and when its plain was covered with verdure, and traced with streams, which poured into the ocean, she erected her habitation on the sea-shore.

Not long after, she was delivered of a daughter, and was supported by the spontaneous productions of the earth, till the child arrived to womanhood. She was then solicited in marriage by several animals, changed into the forms of young men; but they were rejected successively by the mother, until the turtle offered himself as a suitor, and was received. After she had laid herself down to sleep, the turtle placed two arrows on her body, in the form of a cross—one headed with flint, the other with the rough bark of a tree. In due time she was delivered of two sons, but died in child-birth.

The grandmother, enraged at her daughter's death, resolved to destroy them, and threw them into the sea. Scarcely had she reached her wigwam, when the children overtook her at the door. She then concluded to let them live; and, dividing the corpse of her daughter in two parts, she threw them up towards the heavens, where one became the sun, the other the moon. Then first began the succession of day and night. The children speedily became men, and expert archers. The elder had the arrow of the turtle which was pointed with flint; the younger had the arrow headed with bark. The former was, by his malignant disposition, and his skill and success in hunting, a favourite with his grandmother. They lived in the midst of plenty, but would not permit the younger brother, whose arrow was insufficient to kill any thing larger than birds, to share in their abundance.

As this young man was wandering one day along the shore, he saw a bird perched on a bough, projecting over the water. He attempted to kill it; but his arrow, till that time unerring, flew wide of the mark, and sank in the sea. He determined to recover it, and plunged to the bottom. Here, to his astonishment, he found himself in a small cottage. A venerable old man, sitting there, received him with a smile, and thus addressed him:— "My son, I welcome you to the habitation of your father! To obtain this interview, I directed all the circumstances which have conspired to bring you hither. Here is your arrow, and here is an ear of corn. I have watched the unkindness of your brother, and command you to take his life. When you return home, collect all the flints you can find, and hang up all the bucks'-horns. These are the only things which will make an impression on his body, which is made of flint."

Having received these instructions, the young man took his leave, and, in a quarrel with his brother, drove him to a distant region, far beyond the Savannahs, in the south-west, where he killed him, and left his huge form of flint on the earth. The great enemy to the race of the turtle being thus destroyed, they sprang from the ground in human form, and multiplied in peace.

The grandmother, roused to furious resentment for the loss of her favourite son, resolved to be revenged. For many days successively she caused the rain to descend from the clouds in torrents, until the whole surface of the earth, and even the highest mountains, were covered. The inhabitants escaped by fleeing to their canoes. She then covered the earth with snow; but they betook themselves to their snow-shoes. She then gave up the hope of destroying them at once, and has ever since employed herself in inflicting lesser evils on the world, while her younger son displays his benevolence by showering blessings on his race.

The reader will have traced the analogy between this and the Scripture account of the deluge, &c.

UTICA.

This long tradition has left us little room for Utica, which truly is among those spots (said to be the happiest in the world) with no striking events in its history. It is a pretty and thriving town, half way between Lake Ontario and the Susquehanna, and on the great routes by canal, road, and rail-road, to the west; and in the centre of these radii of communication is fast becoming a focus of wealth and refinement. A high reputation for the latter, however, its society has long and deservedly enjoyed.

THE LANDING ON THE AMERICAN SIDE.

61

(FALLS OF NIAGARA.)

The cliff and staircase at this Landing would be considered highly picturesque any where but at the side of Niagara. The hundred stairs clinging to the rock, the wild vines overgrowing the temporary shed under which travellers take shelter from the spray, the descending and ascending figures, and the athletic boatmen, whose occupation of pulling across this troubled ferry requires herculean strength and proportions, all form a subject for the painter, which could only be disregarded amid the engrossing scenes of Niagara.

There is another staircase extending down the precipitous front of Goat Island, between the two cataracts, which is less picturesque in itself, but much more daring in its position. One marvels at first how it ever was constructed; but a story told in an old book of travels, published in London in 1750, shows that human feet have stood on the isolated and quaking cliff below, and returned again to the summit without the aid of mechanical science. The narrator is a Mr. Peter Kalm, a Swedish gentleman, then on his travels in America:—

"It was formerly thought impossible for any body living to come at the island that is in the middle of the Fall; but an accident that happened twelve years ago made it appear otherwise. The history is this:—Two Indians of the Six Nations went out from Niagara Fort to hunt upon an island that is in the middle of the river, or strait, some miles above the great Fall, on which there used to be abundance of deer. They took some French brandy with them from the fort, which they tasted several times as they were carrying their canoe around the Fall; and when they were in the canoe, they now and then took a dram, and so went along up the strait toward the island where they proposed to hunt; but growing sleepy, they laid themselves down in the canoe, which getting loose, drove back with the stream farther and farther down, till it came nigh that island that is in the middle of the Fall. Here, one of them, awakened by the noise, cries out to the other that they were gone!—yet they tried if possible to save life. This island between the Falls was nighest, and with much working they got there. At first, they were glad; but when they had considered every thing, they thought themselves hardly in a better state than if they had gone down the Fall, since they had now no other choice than either to throw themselves down the same, or to perish with hunger: but hard necessity put them on invention. At the lower end of the island the rock is perpendicular, and there is a break in the fall. The island having plenty of wood, they went to work directly and made a ladder, or shrouds, of the bark of linden tree, which is very tough and strong, so long, that it would reach to the edge of the water below. One end of this bark ladder they tied fast to a great tree that grew at the side of the rock above the Fall, and let the other end down to the water.

"So they went down their new-invented stairs; and when they came to the bottom in the middle of the Fall, they rested a little; and as the water next below the Fall is not rapid, they threw themselves out into it, thinking to swim on shore. Hardly had the Indians began to swim, before the waves of the eddy threw them with violence against the rock from whence they started. They tried it several times, but at last were weary, and being often thrown against the rock they were much bruised, and the skin of their bodies torn in many places. So they were obliged to climb up their stairs again to the island, not knowing what to do. After some time they perceived Indians on the opposite shore, to whom they cried out. These two pitied them, but gave them little hopes of help; yet they made haste down to the fort, and told the French commander where two of their brethren were. He persuaded them to try all possible means of relieving the two poor Indians; and it was done in this manner. The water that runs on the east side of the island is shallow, and breaks in rapids over the rocks. The commandant caused poles to be made and pointed with iron: two Indians determined to walk to this island by the help of these poles to save the others, or perish. They took leave of their friends as if they were going to death. Each had two such poles in his hands to set against the bottom of the stream to keep them steady: so they went and got to the island, and having given poles to the poor Indians there, they all returned safely to the main. The unfortunate creatures had been nine days on the island, and were almost starved to death."

A bridge is now thrown across where these adventurous Indians made their passage. If the story be true, it is one of the most gallant feats on record.

VIEW FROM MOUNT WASHINGTON.

Of two attempts to obtain a view from the summit of Mount Washington, the MS. Journal from which we have already made extracts, gives an interesting account of one which the weather rendered unsuccessful.

"The morning opened with every symptom of a fine day for the ascent. We had an early breakfast, and started a little before six, with the intention of first ascending Mount Clinton, and afterwards Mount Washington. Before we came to the peak of Clinton, however, a thick mist had swept over the mountains, which grew heavier and heavier. At the beginning of the granite pile that caps Mount Washington, a heavy wind with violent rain came on, and, as we climbed upwards, the storm increased, and the cold became every moment more intense. In four hours we reached the summit, thoroughly drenched, and stiff as icicles. The rain beat across the peak with tremendous force, and it was with difficulty we could stand. Below us was a sea of mist, around us a howling tempest, and our only resource was to seek the shelter of a rock, and seek consolation in the guide's knapsack. Though my hands were so benumbed with cold, and my limbs so heavy with the water which had been driven into every thread of my dress that I could hardly raise the food to my lips, I contrived to cut the cork of a bottle of champagne, and its sparkling contents sent a momentary and grateful thrill through my veins: when it had passed, however, I was colder than ever.

"We found so few attractions on the mountain that we soon began our descent towards Ethan Crawford's, but were so blinded by the tempest that the guide could not at once discover the way. Half an hour we wandered about in absolute uncertainty whether we should get down the mountain, or bide the peltings of the storm through the night. We hit at last upon the path, and after some sharp scrambling reached the wood, the friendly shelter of which afforded us a most welcome protection from the rain. The path was execrable, owing to the heavy rain, and the trampling of the horses of another party who had gone up before us; but at four we arrived at our destination, tired, cold, wet, and hungry. A change of dress, a roaring fire, and a substantial dinner, soon put us in better condition and humour."

From a more successful attempt by the same gentleman, we take the following description of the view from Mount Washington.

"The light streamed down through breaks in the clouds on the scenery below in such masses, and in such a manner, as to bring out fully and distinctly all the leading points in the immeasurable panorama. In our immediate neighbourhood, but far below us, lay on one side, Mounts Clinton, Pleasant, Monroe, and Franklin; on the other, Jefferson, Adams, and Madison. On the east and west, openings were visible, through which several rivers, taking their rise in the mountains, wound their way and widened their valleys toward the lowlands. Far in the distance, chains of hills and mountains, distinct in outline and beautiful in form, arose on all sides; and these were still overtopped by others beyond, whose blue summits mingled with the sky, and shut in the overpowering scene. Far to the south, the bright sheet of Lake Winipiseogee met the eye, and with its calm and gem-like beauty, set, as it were, in a frame-work of distant hills, relieved and contrasted the bewildering and boundless majesty which encircled the mountain. On the west the green mountains of Vermont, and on the east the mountains of Maine, skirted the horizon, and seemed to support the heavens. Occasionally, a cloud would rest for a few moments on some distant or neighbouring summit, but during the whole of our visit the awful head of Mount Washington was surrounded by a pure atmosphere and the clearest light."

Mount Washington was ascended by several scientific gentlemen in July, 1784. The historian of the expedition records that one of the company had taken a thermometer from his bosom, when it stood at fever heat, and it fell to 44°; and that, during the time he was adjusting a barometer and thermometer, the cold nearly deprived him of the use of his fingers.

MOUNT WASHINGTON AND THE WHITE HILLS.
(FROM NEAR CRAWFORD'S.)

The White Hills have a double claim to their title—one founded upon the fact, that, for nine, ten, and sometimes eleven months in the year, they are covered with snow; and the other, that, in all clear days, (the only times in which they can be distinctly seen,) white fleecy clouds resting upon them, give them a white aspect. When viewed from a neighbouring position, they are always, except where snow lies, or the rocks are naked, shrouded in misty azure.

The height of these mountains has been a subject of much dispute. A scientific gentleman, whose remarks on physical subjects merit consideration and respect, supposes the summit of Mount Washington to be about seven thousand eight hundred feet above the level of the ocean; seventy-two feet below the point, which, in the latitude of 44° 15′ (that of these mountains) is the estimated point of perpetual congelation on the eastern continent. This point, he says, from the greater coldness of the American climate, cannot exceed, but must rather fall short, of what it is in the European climate. The climates of America are indeed colder than those of Europe in the same latitude during the winter, but in the summer they are generally much hotter. Nor are the mountains in any part of New England of sufficient height and extent to lessen materially the degree of heat generally prevailing. The air on the summit of Mount Washington, therefore, must continually be rendered less cold by the ascent of the intensely heated atmosphere from the subjacent regions. As the whole country partakes of this heat, the ascending volume, whencesoever derived, must be heated to nearly the same temperature. It seems scarcely credible, therefore, that the temperature of the atmosphere around the single point of Mount Washington should not, during the summer, be sensibly raised by the general heat of the country: for we are to remember that this is the only height in the United States which approximates near to the region of perpetual frost.

The following observations of Dr. Cutler exhibit the state of vegetation on these mountains:—

"At the base of the summit of Mount Washington, the limits of vegetation may with propriety be fixed. There are indeed, on some of the rocks, even to their apices, scattered specks of a mossy appearance; but I conceive them to be extraneous substances accidentally adhering to the rocks, for I could not discover, with my botanical microscope, any part of that plant regularly formed. The limits of vegetation at the base of this summit are as well defined as that between the woods and the bald and mossy part. So striking is the appearance, that, at a considerable distance, the mind is impressed with the idea that vegetation extends no farther than a line, as well defined as the penumbra and shadow in a lunar eclipse. The stones that I have by me from the summit have not the smallest appearance of moss upon them.

"There is evidently the appearance of three zones—the woods, the bald, mossy part, and the part above vegetation. The same appearance has been observed on the Alps, and all other high mountains.

"I recollect no grass on the plain. The spaces between the rocks in the second zone and on the plain are filled with spruce and fir, which, perhaps, have been growing ever since the deluge; and yet many of them have not attained a greater height than three or four inches; but their spreading tops are so thick and strong as to support the weight of a man without yielding in the slightest degree. In many places on the sides we could get glades of this growth some rods in extent, when we could, by sitting down on our feet, slide the whole length. The tops of the growth of wood were so thick and firm as to bear us currently a considerable distance before we arrived at the utmost boundaries, which were almost as well defined as the water on the shore of a pond. The tops of the wood had the appearance of having been shorn off, exhibiting a smooth surface from their upper limits to a great distance down the mountains."

On the summit of Mount Washington there is usually little or no snow. That which is so long visible in the regions below is blown from the summit, and the north-western side, and lies only on the southern and south-eastern, where it is defended from every cold wind by the precipice above, and exposed through June, July, and sometimes a part of August, to the full strength of the sun.

THE PARK AND CITY HALL, NEW YORK.

The first Stadt Huys in this city was constructed of stone, and stood originally at the head of Coenties Slip, facing on Pearl Street, towards the East river. It was built as early in the Dutch dynasty as 1642, and became so weakened and impaired in half a century afterwards, that the court sitting there recommended it to be sold, and another to be constructed. In 1699, they sold the old building for nine hundred and twenty pounds, "reserving only the bell, the king's arms, and iron works (fetters) belonging to the prison." By the agreement, leave was granted "that the cage, pillory, and stocks, before the same, be removed any time within one year, and the prisoners in the city hall to remain one month." "In front of all these, on the river, was placed the Rondeal, or Half-Moon Fort, where it probably assisted the party sheltered in the City Hall, while the civil war prevailed."

The new building must have been finished in 1700. It stood at the head of Broad Street, fronting on Wall Street; and its lower story formed an open arcade over the foot pavement. It was also the proper prison of the city, and had before it, on Broad Street, a whipping-post, pillory, &c. There were also held the sessions of the Provincial Assembly, the Supreme Court, and the Mayor and Admiralty Courts. It was finally altered to suit the Congress; and at that time the prisoners were moved to the new jail in the park; but the Congress removing to Philadelphia, it was again altered to receive the courts and the State Assembly.

"It was in the gallery of the old City Hall, on Wall Street," says Watson in his Annals, "that General Washington was inaugurated the first President of the United States. The oath of office was taken in the open gallery in front of the Senate Chamber, in the view of an immense concourse of citizens. There this nobleman of nature, with his noble height and port, in a suit of dark silk velvet of the old cut, steel-hilted small sword by his side, hair in bag and full powdered, in black silk hose, and shoes with silver buckles, made his pledge on a quarto Bible, still preserved in St. John's Lodge. How uprightly, intelligently, and disinterestedly, he executed his task, history will never cease to tell to his fame and glory."

The present City Hall was erected in 1803, at an expense of half a million of dollars. The front and sides are constructed of white marble, and the remainder of red sandstone. It is a beautiful edifice, and only wants elevation. When the trees of the park are in full leaf, it is difficult to get an entire view of it.

The park is the centre of New York, and its two most thronged and finest avenues form the two sides of it. Broadway, the much crowded and much praised Broadway, the Corso, the Toledo, the Regent Street, of New York, pours its tide of population past the western side of the verdant triangle, and, just at the park, its crowd and its bustle are thickest. Broadway is a noble street, and on its broad side-walks may be seen every thing that walks the world in the shape of a foreigner, or a fashion—beauties by the score, and men of business by the thousand; but, besides every possible ingredient of continental crowds, there are to be seen in Broadway two additional classes of peripatetics seen never on foreign pavés but in rare specimens—coloured dandies, and belligerent pigs. The former take the wall of you, and the latter, when the question of passing on one side or the other becomes embarrassing, escape with great dexterity between your legs.

It would be difficult in one day to describe the prevailing style of dress in Broadway, for fashions have become unfashionable, and each man and woman dresses as Fortune pleases. But here is a picture of dresses in Broadway a century ago:—

"Men wore three-square, or cocked hats, and wigs; coats with large cuffs, and big skirts lined and stiffened with buckram. The coat of a beau had three or four large plaits in the skirts, and wadding, like a coverlet, to keep them smooth. The cuffs were very large, up to the elbows, open below, and loaded with lead to keep them down. The cape was thin and low, so as readily to expose the close-plaited neck-stock of fine linen cambric, and the large silver stock-buckle on the back of the neck. The shirts were worn with hand-ruffles, and sleeve-buttons were worn at the wrist, of precious stones, or gold. The little boys wore wigs, like their elders, and their dresses generally were similar to those of the men. Coats of red plush were very fashionable, and the breeches were commonly made of this material."

We refer the reader to Watson's Annals for many curious particulars touching the apparel and habits of the New Yorkers in the early part of the last century.

THE TWO LAKES AND THE MOUNTAIN HOUSE
ON THE CATSKILLS.

At this elevation, you may wear woollen and sleep under blankets in midsummer; and that is a pleasant temperature where much hard work is to be done in the way of pleasure-hunting. No place so agreeable as Catskill, after one has been parboiled in the city. New York is at the other end of that long thread of a river, running away south from the base of the mountain; and you may change your climate in so brief a transit, that the most enslaved broker in Wall Street may have half his home on Catskill. The cool woods, the small silver lakes, the falls, the mountain-tops, are all delicious haunts for the idler-away of the hot months; and, to the credit of our taste, it may be said they are fully improved—Catskill is a "resort."

From the Mountain-House, the busy and all-glorious Hudson is seen winding half its silver length—towns, villas, and white spires, sparkling on the shores, and snowy sails and gaily-painted steamers, specking its bosom. It is a constant diorama of the most lively beauty; and the traveller, as he looks down upon it, sighs to make it a home. Yet a smaller and less-frequented stream would best fulfil desires born of a sigh. There is either no seclusion on the Hudson, or there is so much that the conveniences of life are difficult to obtain. Where the steamers come to shore, (twenty a day, with each from one to seven hundred passengers,) it is certainly far from secluded enough; yet, away from the landing-places, servants find your house too lonely, and your table, without unreasonable expense and trouble, is precarious and poor. These mean and menus plaisirs reach, after all, the very citadel of philosophy. Who can live without a cook or a chambermaid, and dine seven days in the week on veal, consoling himself with the beauties of a river-side?

On the smaller rivers these evils are somewhat ameliorated; for in the rural and uncorrupt villages of the interior, you may find servants born on the spot, and content to live in the neighbourhood. The market is better, too, and the society less exposed to the evils that result from too easy an access to the metropolis. No place can be rural, in all the virtues of the phrase, where a steamer will take the villager to the city between noon and night, and bring him back between midnight and morning. There is a suburban look and character about all the villages on the Hudson which seems out of place among such scenery. They are suburbs; in fact, steam has destroyed the distance between them and the city.

The Mountain-House on the Catskill, it should be remarked, is a luxurious hotel. How the proprietor can have dragged up, and keeps dragging up, so many superfluities from the river level to that eagle's nest, excites your wonder. It is the more strange, because in climbing a mountain the feeling is natural that you leave such enervating indulgences below. The mountain-top is too near heaven. It should be a monastery to lodge in so high—a St. Gothard, or a Vallambrosa. But here you may choose between Hermitages, "white" or "red," Burgundies, Madeiras, French dishes, and French dances, as if you had descended upon Capua.

TRENTON HIGH FALLS.

Those who visit these Falls in the pleasantest season for travelling, (the time at which the drawing was taken by Mr. Bartlett,) see them when there is the least water; consequently, when they are (as falls) at their lesser phase of grandeur. It is like seeing a race-horse in the stall, or a line-of-battle-ship in port, with sails furled. It is possible that after one of the tremendous thunder-storms which burst upon this climate sometimes in summer, the glory of the cataract may, for a few hours, renew, and so unite the splendour of full foliage with the flashing of mighty waters: but this is a chance which the traveller for pleasure will scarce hit or wait for. It should be remembered, however, in looking on the drawing, that it is one of a sleeping lion. The frowning walls on either side, driven asunder by the plunges of the torrent in more "yeasty moods," present a sufficient scale by which to measure its slumbering power. Those who live in climes where snow seldom falls, and more seldom lies through one sunny day unmelted, can have but a faint idea of a spring freshet in America. After the first heavy snow in December, each successive fall adds solidity to the heap upon the earth's bosom, and the alternate thawing and freezing consolidates the bottom into ice, and cuts off the heat of the soil from the flakes added almost daily to the surface. Till the middle of March, perhaps, or later, the sleighing (Anglicè sledging) is hard and crisp. Then the sun draws towards the line, and with the equinox come soft southern winds, with sharp changes to the north, pouring sleet and rain upon the crusty covering of nature; and, first of all, the small streams begin to trickle under the ice, smothered and faint; the roads across the hard-frozen rivers crack and grow treacherous; and the horse, as they phrase it here, slumps through in travelling on the highway. As the days grow longer, the snow gets clammy and heavy, and drops to the

67

ground, (undermined by the water,) an acre at a time, clicking like a troop of morris-dancers. If you "sit upon a rail" at noon-day, and send a dog to run over an untrodden field, his weight will break it down in large tablets, like the giving way of a marble floor. Then comes the spring thaw. Instead of one rivulet to half a mile, every hill-side sends down a hundred streams, every road is a brook, every hollow in the fields an overflowing pond. The benevolent societies which thrive more by the "widows' mites" than the rich man's gift, have learned the secret of these "small contributions." Down they pour, in troops of legions, to the beds of the larger water-courses, "drowning the springs," overflowing the banks, and laying every low plain under water. The ice crashes and loosens in the large rivers, and with the loosening of their frost-bound chains, the merry dance is led off to the ocean. If you would see waterfalls, it should be then; though the foliage is not around them, nor the sky or the moon-light so genial above. Niagara alone, of all the cataracts, remains unchanged. He rolls on in his calm sublimity, spring and autumn, summer and winter, the same. His floods seem never to increase by the melting of snow, nor to be drunk up by the fervour of the sun. If changes he has, they are imperceptible, or seen only in the crumbling of rock beneath him, mountains at a convulsion, and at intervals of years.

Trenton is in a wild and not very accessible part of the country, else it were worth the while of the traveller to see these fine Falls during the spring. I am very sure that a series of sketches upon the same ground—the same scenes by the same artist, done when the waters are at the flood, would not be recognised as at all resembling. The attempt would be curious to the artist, at least.

VALLEY OF THE SHENANDOAH,
FROM JEFFERSON'S ROCK.

This is one of the most harmonious combinations of mountain, vale, and river, to be found in America; we know not whether to call it more beautiful or grand. Fine as is all the scenery of this neighbourhood, however, it is not till very lately that the current of travel has turned thither, and but partially yet. Harper's Ferry will soon be a resort for admirers of nature from all nations, and it may well share the honours of pilgrimage with Trenton Falls and Niagara. Steam navigation across the Atlantic will make our New World lions as tame as the Pyramids.

It is difficult, at least for me, to stand on any eminence commanding a landscape, wild, yet formed for a blest human residence, without seeing in it the forfeited inheritance of the red man. The unpicturesque new village of the white man, his mill, or his factory, does not convey to my imagination an image of happiness; and I regret the primitive rover of the wild, who neither blackened nature with smoke, nor violated her harmony with brick and shingle. The tide of sympathy seems turning of late against these oppressed tribes, and it is not amiss sometimes to remember our own atrocities as well as theirs. What will be thought hereafter of the massacre of the poor Conestogoes, as related in the history of these middle regions of our territory!

"On the first arrival of the English," says the chronicler, "messengers from this tribe entered into a treaty of friendship with the first proprietary, William Penn, which was to last as long as the sun should shine, or the waters run in the rivers.

"This treaty has been since frequently renewed, and the chain brightened, as they express it, from time to time. It has never been violated on their part, or ours, till now. As their lands by degrees were mostly purchased, and the settlement of the white people began to surround them, the proprietor assigned them lands on the manor of Conestogoe, which they might not part with; there they have lived many years in friendship with their white neighbours, who loved them for their peaceable inoffensive behaviour.

"It has always been observed, that Indians, settled in the neighbourhood of white people, do not increase, but diminish continually. This tribe accordingly went on diminishing, till there remained in their town on the manor but twenty persons, namely, seven men, five women, and eight children, boys and girls.

"Of these, Shehaes was a very old man, having assisted at the second treaty held with them by Mr. Penn, in 1701, and ever since continued a faithful friend to the English; he is said to have been an exceeding good man, considering his education, being naturally of a kind, benevolent temper.

"This little society continued the custom they had begun, when more numerous, of addressing every new governor, and every descendant of the first proprietary, welcoming him to the province, assuring him of their fidelity, and praying a continuance of that favour and protection which they had hitherto experienced. They had accordingly sent up an address of this kind to our present governor (John Penn, Esq.) on his arrival; but the same was scarcely delivered, when the unfortunate catastrophe happened which we are about to relate. On Wednesday, the 14th December, 1763, fifty-seven men from some of our frontier townships, who had projected the destruction of this little commonwealth, came all well mounted, and armed with firelocks, hangers, and hatchets, having travelled through the country in the night to Conestogoe manor. There they surrounded the small village of Indian huts, and just at break of day broke in upon them all at once. Only three men, two women, and a young boy, were found at home; the rest being out among the neighbouring white people—some to sell the baskets, brooms, and bowls, they manufactured, and others on other occasions. These poor defenceless creatures were immediately fired upon, stabbed, and hatcheted to death! the good Shehaes among the rest cut to pieces in his bed!—all of them were scalped, and otherwise horribly mangled. Then their huts were set on fire, and most of them burned down. The magistrates of Lancaster sent out to collect the remaining Indians, brought them into the town for their better security against any further attempt, and, it is said, condoled with them on the misfortune that had happened, took them by the hand, and promised them protection. They were put into the workhouse, a strong building, as the place of greatest safety. These cruel men again assembled themselves; and hearing that the remaining fourteen Indians were in the workhouse at Lancaster, they suddenly appeared before that town on the 27th December. Fifty of them, armed as before, dismounting, went directly to the workhouse, and, by violence, broke open the door, and entered with the utmost fury in their countenances. When the poor wretches saw they had no protection nigh, nor could possibly escape, and being without the least weapon of defence, they divided their little families, the children clinging to their parents; they fell on their faces, protested their innocence, declared their love to the English, and that, in their whole lives, they had never done them injury; and in this posture they all received the hatchet! Men, women, and children, were every one inhumanly murdered in cold blood!"

LOCKPORT—ERIE CANAL.

This town, so suddenly sprung into existence, is about thirty miles from Lake Erie, and exhibits one of those wonders of enterprise which astonish calculation. The waters of Lake Erie, which have come thus far without much descent, are here let down sixty feet by five double locks, and thence pursue a perfectly level course, sixty-five miles, to Rochester. The remarkable thing at Lockport, however, is a deep cut from here to the Torenanta Creek, seven miles in length, and partly through solid rock, at an average depth of twenty feet. The canal boat glides through this flinty bed, with jagged precipices on each side; and the whole route has very much the effect of passing through an immense cavern.

This tract of country is very interesting to the antiquarian, from the remains of fortifications, and other probable traces of a race who existed, and whose arts perished before the occupation of the country by the tribes who lately possessed it. On Seneca river, on the south side of Lake Erie, in many different parts of the State of New York, and in a long chain extending west through the valley of the Ohio, down that of the Mississippi, and so westward through Mexico, are traces of a people who were settled in towns defended by forts, and altogether far more advanced in civilization than the Iroquois found here by Europeans. The region in the neighbourhood of Lockport and Torenanta was visited with reference to these remains by the Rev. Mr. Kirkland, missionary to the Iroquois confederacy, in 1778. His account is very curious. At a deserted Indian village, near the old Indian town of Kanawageas, he discovered an ancient fort. It enclosed about six acres, and had six gates. The ditch appeared to be eight feet wide, and in some places six feet deep, and drawn in a circular form on three sides. The fourth side was defended by nature with a high bank, at the foot of which is a fine stream of water. The bank had probably been secured by a stockade, as there appeared to have been a deep covered way in the middle of it down to the water. Some of the trees on the bank and in the ditch appeared to Mr. Kirkland to have been at the age of two hundred years. About half a mile south of this, and upon a greater eminence, he traced the ruins of another old fortified town, of less dimensions than the other, but with a deeper ditch, and in a situation more lofty and defensible. Having examined these fortifications, Mr. Kirkland returned to Kanawageas, and thence renewed his tour westward, until he encamped for the night at a place called Joàika, (i.e. Racoon,) on the river Tanawànde, about twenty-six miles from Kanawangeas. Six miles from this place of encampment, he rode to the open fields, and arrived at a place called by the Senecas Tegatàinèáaghgwe, which imports a double-fortified town, or a town with a fort at each end. Here he walked about half a mile with one of the Seneca chiefs, to view one of the vestiges of this double-fortified town: they were the remains of two forts. The first which he visited, as above, contained about four acres of ground: the other to which he proceeded, distant from this about two miles, and situated at the other extremity of the ancient town, enclosed twice that quantity of ground. The ditch around the former, which he particularly examined, was about five or six feet deep. A small stream of water and a high bank circumscribed nearly one-third of the enclosed ground. There were the traces of six gates, or avenues, round the ditch; and near the centre a way was dug to the water. The ground on the opposite side of the water was in some places nearly as high as that on which the fort was built, which might render this covered way to the water necessary. A considerable number of large thrifty oaks had grown up within the enclosed ground, both in and upon the ditch; some of them appeared to be at least two hundred years old, or more. The ground is of a hard gravelly kind, intermixed with loam, and more plentifully at the brow of the hill. In some places, at the bottom of the ditch, Mr. Kirkland ran his cane a foot or more into the ground, from which circumstance he concluded that the ditch was much deeper in its original state than it then appeared to him. Near the northern fortification, which was situated on high ground, he found the remains of a funeral pile, where the slain were buried, in a great battle, which will be spoken of hereafter. The earth was raised about six feet above the common surface, and betwixt twenty and thirty feet diameter. The bones appeared on the whole surface of the raised earth, and struck out in many places on the sides. Pursuing his course towards Buffalo Creek, (his ultimate destination,) Mr. Kirkland

70

discovered the vestiges of another ancient fortified town. He does not in his manuscript delineate them, but, from the course he described, they might be easily ascertained. "Upon these heights, near the ancient fortified town, the roads part; we left the path leading to Niagara on our right, and went a course nearly south-west for Buffalo Creek. After leaving these heights, which afforded an extensive prospect, we travelled over a fine tract of land for about six or seven miles; then came to a barren white oak-shrub plain, and one very remarkable spot of near two hundred acres, and passed a steep hill on our right, in some places near fifty feet perpendicular, at the bottom of which is a small lake, affording another instance of pagan superstition. The old Indians affirm that, formerly, a demon, in the form of a dragon, resided in this lake, and had frequently been seen to disgorge balls of liquid fire; and that, to appease his wrath, many a sacrifice of tobacco had been made at that lake by the fathers. The barren spot above mentioned is covered with small white stone, that appears like lime and clay; in some spots, for a considerable distance, there is no appearance of earth. Notwithstanding its extreme poverty, there are many trees of moderate size. At the extremity of this barren plain, we came again to the Tanawande river, and forded it about two miles above the Indian town called by that name. This village contains fourteen houses, or huts; their chief is called Gashagaàle, nicknamed the black chief. On the south side of the Tanawande Creek, at a small distance, are to be seen the vestiges of another ancient fortified town." Mr. Kirkland further remarks, that there are vestiges of ancient fortified towns in various parts throughout the extensive territory of the Six Nations, and, by Indian report, in various other parts; particularly one on a branch of the Delaware river, which, from the size and age of some of the trees that have grown upon the banks and in the ditches, appears to have existed nearly one thousand years.

THE TOMB OF WASHINGTON.
MOUNT VERNON.

The current of life seems to be too rapid in America to allow time for reflection upon any thing which can possibly be deferred. The monuments are left unfinished on our battle-fields; the tombs of great men become indistinguishable before marked with a stone; and the sacred places where patriotism has dwelt, are rated by the value of their material, and left to decay. It is difficult to visit Mount Vernon, and feel, from any mark of care or respect visible about it, that America owes any thing to the sacred ashes it entombs.

The family tomb at Mount Vernon has once been robbed by a sacrilegious ruffian, whose ignorance alone preserved for us the remains of Washington. It has been proposed to Congress to buy Mount Vernon, and establish a guard over relics so hallowed. Why should not this be done, and a sufficient sum be appropriated to enclose and keep in order the whole estate, improve the execrable road leading to it from Alexandria, and employ persons to conduct strangers over the place?

The vault in which the ashes of Washington repose, is at the distance of, perhaps, thirty rods from the house, immediately upon the bank of the river. A more romantic and picturesque site for a tomb can scarcely be imagined. Between it and the Potomac is a curtain of forest-trees, covering the steep declivity to the water's edge, breaking the glare of the prospect, and yet affording glimpses of the river, where the foliage is thickest. The tomb is surrounded by several large native oaks, which are venerable by their years, and which annually strew the sepulchre with autumnal leaves, furnishing the most appropriate drapery for the place, and giving a still deeper impression to the memento mori. Interspersed among the oaks, and overhanging the tomb, is a copse of red cedar, whose evergreen boughs present a fine contrast to the hoary and leafless branches of the oak; and while the deciduous foliage of the latter indicates the decay of the body, the eternal verdure of the former furnishes a fitting emblem of the immortal spirit. The sacred and symbolic cassia was familiar to Washington, and, perhaps, led to the selection of a spot where the evergreen flourished.

One of the most interesting associations with the tomb of Washington, is La Fayette's visit to it, as related by Levasseur:—

"After a voyage of two hours, the guns of Fort Washington announced that we were approaching the last abode of the father of his country. At this solemn signal, to which the military band accompanying us responded by plaintive strains, we went on deck, and the venerable soil of Mount Vernon was before us. At this view, an involuntary and spontaneous movement made us kneel. We landed in boats, and trod upon the ground so often trod by the feet of Washington. A carriage received General Lafayette; and the other visitors silently ascended the precipitous path which conducted to the solitary habitation of Mount Vernon. In re-entering beneath this hospitable roof, which had sheltered him when the reign of terror tore him violently from his country and family, George Lafayette felt his heart sink within him, at no more finding him whose paternal care had softened his misfortunes; while his father sought with emotion for every thing which reminded him of the companion of his glorious toils.

"Three nephews of General Washington took Lafayette, his son, and myself, to conduct us to the tomb of their uncle: our numerous companions remained in the house. In a few minutes the cannon, thundering anew, announced that Lafayette rendered homage to the ashes of Washington. Simple and modest as he was during life, the tomb of the citizen hero is scarcely perceived among the sombre cypresses by which it is surrounded. A vault, slightly elevated and dodded over—a wooden door without inscriptions—some withered and green garlands, indicate to the traveller who visits the spot, where rest in peace the puissant arms which broke the chains of his country. As we approached, the door was opened. Lafayette descended alone into the vault, and a few minutes after re-appeared, with his eyes overflowing with tears. He took his son and me by the hand, and led us into the tomb, where, by a sign, he indicated the coffin. We knelt reverentially, and rising, threw ourselves into the arms of Lafayette, and mingled our tears with his."

BLACK MOUNTAIN—LAKE GEORGE.

The mountains on the shore of this exquisite lake consist of two great ranges, bordering it from north to south. The western range passes westward of the north-west bay, at the head of which a vast spar, shooting towards the south-east, forms the whole of the peninsula between that bay and the lake. Both these ranges alternately approach the lake, so as to constitute a considerable part of its shores, and recede from it again to the distance sometimes of two or three miles.

The summits of these mountains are of almost every figure, from the arch, to the bold, bluff, and sharp cone. In some instances, the loftier ones are bald, solemn, and forbidding; in others, they are clothed and crowned with verdure. It is the peculiarity of Lake George, that, while all the world agrees to speak only of its loveliness, it is surrounded by features of the highest grandeur and sublimity. The Black Mountain is one of these; and there is every variety of chasm, crag, promontory, and peak, which a painter would require for the noblest composition of mountain scenery. The atmospheric changes here, too, are almost always violent; and storms are so frequent, that there is scarce a traveller to Lake George in the summer who has not seen it in a thunder-storm.

It was remarked to me on this lake by a foreigner, that, with all the luxuriance of the vegetation, the trees seemed small; and it is a remark that is frequently made by Englishmen, who compare the common trees in the woods on the roadside with the oaks left to flourish for centuries in venerating and venerable England. The best answer to this remark is contained in a letter, addressed to a friend in England, by an able writer of this country:—

"The soil of New England is naturally quite as rich and productive as that of England: of this the thrifty growth and ultimate size of our forest-trees is ample proof. Few of them, indeed, can now be found of this size: almost all the original forests of this country having been long since cut down. I have seen many of these trees, and have compared them with the accounts given of forests in many parts of the globe, and am assured that they will very rarely suffer by such comparison. It may seem strange to you, accustomed as you are to see forest-trees planted in great numbers, and preserved with great care, that the inhabitants of this country should, so soon after its colonization, have cut down their forests in this extensive manner. This is one of the ten thousand subjects, presented to the mind by the existing state of things here, about which a foreigner must necessarily misconceive. Should he travel through New England he would naturally conclude that the forest-trees failed of arriving at the size which they attain in Europe. He would, indeed, see that they were tall, and apparently very thrifty, but small in the girth. I do not mean that they are universally so; but that this is extensively the fact throughout the southern division. For the reason of it he would be at a loss, and most probably would attribute it, notwithstanding the thrifty appearance of the trees, to sterility of soil, or, in the mystic language of Buffon, to 'a deficiency of matter.' Should he be informed that the real cause was the age of the trees, almost all of which are young, his perplexity would be increased. On the one hand he would be astonished at the folly of destroying forests in this wanton manner, without any apparent reason; and, on the other, would be unable to comprehend how these forests renewed themselves without the aid of planting. All this is, however, easily explicable. The wood of this country is its fuel. An Englishman who sees the various fires of his own country sustained by peat and coal only, cannot easily form a conception of the quantity of wood, or, if you please, of forest which is necessary for this purpose. To this quantity must be added the timber for the uses of building, in a country where almost all buildings are formed merely of timber; of fencing, furniture, and commerce; and a prodigious mass annually destroyed in the recent settlements for the mere purpose of clearing the ground. With these facts before him, he will cease to wonder that forests are very extensively felled in New England. All these forests renew themselves. The seeds of the forest-trees spring more readily and successfully when left on the surface than when buried in the ground, even at a very small depth. They will not, however, germinate upon a sward: they demand a soil loose and light. In this state the soil is always kept in forested ground by the leaves deposited on the earth. These also supply the necessary moisture for germination, and effectually shelter the seeds, particularly the nuts and acorns, from the ravages of animals. In this manner, and by a process totally superior to any contrived by the human mind, forests are furnished by the Author of nature with the means of perpetual self-restoration.

"But this is not the only mode, nor the most expeditious, nor that which is principally relied on in this country. When a field of wood is, in the language of our farmers, cut clean—i.e. when every tree is cut down, so far as any progress is made, vigorous shoots sprout from every stump; and having their nourishment supplied by the roots of the former tree, grow with a thrift and rapidity never seen in stems derived from the seed. Good grounds will thus yield a growth amply sufficient for fuel, once in fourteen years. A multitude of farmers, therefore, cut their wood in this manner; although, it must be confessed, there are different opinions and practices concerning the subject. In these two modes the forests in New England become, in a sense, ever-living, and supply plentifully the wants of the inhabitants."

CONNECTICUT VALLEY, FROM MOUNT HOLYOKE.

The broad open lands, or intervals, as they are called in this country, which border upon the Connecticut, contain some of the most sunny and fertile pictures of cultivation to be found on our continent. From the mouth of the river up to its rise beyond the White Mountains, it is gemmed with beautiful rural towns, many of them among the first in our country for prosperity, neatness, and cultivated society.

The history of these towns presents some of the bloodiest traits marked on the early settlements of New England. The event which gave the name to Bloody Brook, a small village near the southern extremity of Dresfield, is among many sanguinary records of the difficulties and dangers of the first settlers in this valley.

For a considerable number of years the inhabitants of the valley had lived in as perfect harmony with the Indians among whom they had settled, as was possible, with the great difference between their characters, principles, and pursuits. They had purchased their lands at an equitable price, and in all their transactions with them had observed the strictest equity and humanity. This state of tranquillity was only disturbed by the wide-spreading intrigues of the bold sachem, Philip, whose discernment, comprehensiveness of views, and admirable address, entitle him to the first rank of superiority among the aborigines known in our history. By means of emissaries, and personal solicitation, and eloquence, this renowned warrior succeeded in uniting all the numerous tribes of Indians within the territories colonized by the whites, in one extensive conspiracy of extermination. Though divided into many tribes, hostile to each other and perpetually at war, they joined in this common cause, and a general war broke out at once in every part of the country.

The first symptom in the Valley of the Connecticut, was an abandonment by the Indians of their fortresses and houses. They were pursued by a party of settlers, and overtaken about eight miles above Hatfield; where a skirmish ensued, in which nine or ten whites were killed, and about twenty-six Indians.

Several attacks upon the settlements in the valley immediately followed, repelled always with loss of life; and on the 30th of May, 1676, a body of six or seven hundred attacked Hatfield again. The men were abroad in the fields, but, reinforced by a small band from Hadley, they broke through the Indians, and joined the families who had fled to the fortified houses for protection. After a prolonged contest, they succeeded in driving the Indians from the settlement, which was never again attacked.

The village of Deerfield was among those which had suffered most from the first incursions of the Indians, the houses having been burnt, and the town evacuated in consequence. Their harvest had been cut about two months before, and having been stacked in the fields, escaped the conflagration. About eighty men from the settlements below came up to protect the harvesters in carting it in, and about three thousand bushels of wheat were thrashed, loaded upon the waggons, and had been drawn as far as the brook before mentioned without molestation. The settlers stopped here to gather grasses, and while thus occupied, were suddenly and furiously attacked by a body of eight hundred Indians. Captain Lathrop, the leader of the party, ordered his men to fight the Indians in their own manner, availing themselves of the protection of the trees; but the natives, trained to run from tree to tree, and to conceal themselves in this sort of warfare with

74

unexampled address and caution, fought at great advantage, and soon decided the battle in their own favour. Lathrop was killed at the commencement of the attack; and of the whole number of reapers and armed men, ninety were killed on the spot.

Captain Mosely, who was at Deerfield when the enterprise was undertaken, marched immediately with a small band to the relief of Lathrop; but, when he arrived, the contest was over, and the savages, flushed with success, were pillaging the dead. Forming his men into a close column, and commanding them to keep their ranks, he charged the Indians with the greatest intrepidity. Spite of their numbers, he drove them into a swamp, and forced his way through the whole body. They then attempted to hang upon his rear, but with great presence of mind he wheeled and broke through them again. In this manner the fight was continued for five hours. He drove them several miles, and, with only two men killed, and five or six wounded, succeeded in killing ninety-six of their number, and returned, unmolested, on his way to Deerfield.

The next morning, the little band went out to bury the dead, and found the savages again stripping the bodies on the field of battle. Mosely drove them once more before him, and then, having performed his melancholy task, heaped a monument of loose stones over the victims, and returned. The name of the stream, Bloody Brook, is, at present, the only memorial of the catastrophe.

VIEW ON THE ERIE CANAL, NEAR LITTLE FALLS.

The passage of the Canal, under the lofty bluff which springs at this place from the edge of the Mohawk, is one of the most beautiful of the many beautiful features disclosed to the voyager on this great outlet of the West. No traveller sees a greater variety of fine objects within the same distance than the follower of the Canal from Schenectady to Buffalo; and certainly none sees them with more ease and comfort to himself. The packet-boats are long drawing-rooms, where he dines, sleeps, reads, lolls, or looks out of the window; and if in want of exercise, he may at any time get a quick walk on the tow-path, and all this without perceptible motion, jar, or smell of steam. Of all the modes of travelling in America, the least popular and the most delightful, to our thinking, is travelling on the Canal.

One of the descriptions of scenery through which the Canal passes, and one which is, we believe, peculiar to our country, is what are called openings. When one of these plains is seen at a little distance, a traveller emerging from the forest naturally concludes that it is the commencement of a settled country; and as he advances towards it, is instinctively led to cast his eye forward to find the town or village of which it is the outskirt. From this impression he will be unable to free himself; for though given up, the thought will recur again, spite of his conviction, that he is in the heart of a wilderness. At the same time a sense of stillness and solitude, a feeling of absolute retirement from the world, deeper and more affecting than any he has ever felt before, will be forced upon him while roving in these sequestered regions. No passage out of them is presented to his eye. Yet, though the tract around him is seemingly bounded every where, the boundary is every where obscure, being formed of trees, thinly dispersed, and retired beyond each other at such distances, that, while they actually limit the view, they appear rather to border dim, indistinct openings into other tracts of country. Thus he always feels the limit to be uncertain, and until he is actually leaving one of these plains, will continually expect to find a part of the expansion still spreading beyond the reach of his eye. On every side, a multitude of chasms conduct his eye beyond the labyrinth by which he is surrounded, and present an imaginary passage back into the world from which he is withdrawn, bewildering him with expectation continually awakened to be continually disappointed.

Thus, in a kind of romantic rapture, he wanders over these plains with emotions similar to those with which, when a child, he roamed through the wildernesses created in Arabian tales.

The origin of the peculiar appearance of these grounds, Dr. Dwight supposes, is probably this. The Indians annually, and sometimes oftener, burned such parts of the North American forests as they found sufficiently dry. In every such case, the fuel consists chiefly of the fallen leaves, which are rarely dry enough for an extensive combustion, except on uplands; and on these only when covered with a dry soil. Of this nature were always the oak and yellow pine grounds, which were therefore usually subjected to an annual conflagration. The beech and maple grounds were commonly too wet to be burned. Hence, on these grounds, the vegetable mould is from six inches to a foot in depth, having been rarely or never consumed by fire; while on the oak and pine grounds, it often does not exceed an inch. That this is the effect of fire only, and not of any diversity in the nature of the trees, is evident from the fact, that, in moist soils, where the fire cannot penetrate, the mould is as deep on the oak as on the maple grounds. This mould is combustible, and by an intense fire is wholly consumed.

The object of these conflagrations was to produce fresh and sweet pasture, for the purpose of alluring the deer to the spots on which they had been kindled. Immediately after the fires, a species of grass springs up, sometimes called fire-grass, because it usually succeeds a conflagration. Either from its nature, or from the efficacy of the fire, it is remarkably sweet, and eagerly sought by the deer. All the underwood is at the same time consumed, so that these animals are easily discovered at considerable distances—a thing impracticable where the forests have not been burned. To supply himself with timber for a wigwam, and with wood for fuel, was the only use which the Indian could make of the forest; and the earth furnished him with nothing but a place for his residence, his garden, and his game. While, therefore, he destroyed both the forest and the soil, he converted them to uses most profitable for himself.

When these grounds had been often burned, the seeds and nuts whence future trees would have germinated, were, of course, destroyed by fire. The small number scattered over these plains, or openings, grew on spots which were less ravaged by fire, because they were moist, or because they were less covered with leaves.

HUDSON HIGHLANDS, FROM BULL HILL.

This view out from the gorge of the highlands presents a foreground of cliff and shadow, with their reflections almost folded across in the bosom of the river, and a middle ground of the village of Newburgh and the gently-undulating country in the rear. The blue and far-off line of the Kaatskills shuts in the horizon.

There is some very romantic scenery hidden among the undulations just mentioned, embracing several small rivers, and a romantic stream, called Murderer's Creek, a tributary of the Hudson. Mr. Poulding, in his "New Mirror for Travellers," gives the following interesting legend in explanation of the name:—

"Little more than a century ago, the beautiful region watered by this stream was possessed by a small tribe of Indians, which has long since become extinct, or been incorporated with some other savage nation of the West. Three or four hundred yards from where the stream discharges itself into the Hudson, a white family, of the name of Stacey, had established itself in a log-house, by tacit permission of the tribe, to whom Stacey had made himself useful by his skill in a variety of little arts highly estimated by the savages. In particular, a friendship existed between him and an old Indian, called Naoman, who often came to his house and partook of his hospitality. The Indians never forgive injuries or forget benefits. The family consisted of Stacey, his wife, and two children, a boy and girl, the former five, the latter three years old."

The legend goes on to say, that Naoman, in grateful friendship, gave the wife of Stacey a secret warning, that a massacre of the whites was resolved on, exacting from her a solemn pledge of secrecy, and advising instant escape across the river.

"The daily visits of old Naoman, and his more than ordinary gravity, had excited suspicion in some of the tribe, who had accordingly paid particular attention to the movements of Stacey. One of the young Indians, who had kept on the watch, seeing the whole family about to take their boat, ran to the little Indian village, about a mile off, and gave the alarm. Five Indians collected, ran down to the river side, where their canoes were moored, jumped in, and paddled after Stacey, who by this time had got some distance out into the stream. They gained on him so fast, that twice he dropped his paddle, and took up his gun. But his wife prevented his shooting, by telling him, that if he fired, and they were afterwards overtaken, they would meet no mercy from the Indians. He accordingly refrained, and plied his paddle, till the sweat rolled in big drops down his forehead. All would not do; they were overtaken within a hundred yards of the shore, and carried back with shouts of yelling triumph.

"When they got ashore, the Indians set fire to Stacey's house, and dragged himself, his wife, and children, to their village. Here the principal old men, and Naoman among the rest, assembled to deliberate on the affair. The chief among them stated that some one of the tribe had undoubtedly been guilty of treason, in apprising Stacey, the white man, of the designs of the tribe, whereby they took the alarm, and had well nigh escaped. He proposed to examine the prisoners as to who gave the information. The old men assented to this, and Naoman among the rest. Stacey was first interrogated by one of the old men, who spoke English, and interpreted to the others. Stacey refused to betray his informant. His wife was then questioned, while at the same moment two Indians stood threatening the two children with tomahawks in case she did not confess. She attempted to evade the truth, by declaring she had a dream the night before which had alarmed her, and that she had persuaded her husband to fly. 'The Great Spirit never deigns to talk in dreams to a white face,' said the old Indian: 'woman! thou hast two tongues and two faces: speak the truth, or thy children shall surely die.' The little boy and girl were then brought close to her, and the two savages stood over them, ready to execute their bloody orders.

" 'Wilt thou name,' said the old Indian, 'the red man who betrayed his tribe? I will ask thee three times.' The mother answered not. 'Wilt thou name the traitor? This is the second time.' The poor mother looked at her husband, and then at her children, and stole a glance at Naoman, who sat smoking his pipe with invincible gravity. She wrung her hands and wept, but remained silent. 'Wilt thou name the traitor? 'Tis the third and last time.' The agony of the mother waxed more bitter; again she sought the eye of Naoman, but it was cold and motionless. A pause of a moment awaited her reply, and the next moment the tomahawks were raised over the heads of the children, who besought their mother not to let them be murdered.

" 'Stop!' cried Naoman. All eyes were turned upon him. 'Stop!' repeated he in a tone of authority. 'White woman, thou hast kept thy word with me to the last moment. I am the traitor. I have eaten of the salt, warmed myself at the fire, shared the kindness of these christian white people, and it was I that told them of their danger. I am a withered, leafless, branchless trunk; cut me down if you will. I am ready.' A yell of indignation sounded on all sides. Naoman descended from the little bank where he sat, shrouded his face with his mantle of skins, and submitted to his fate. He fell dead at the feet of the white woman by a blow of the tomahawk."

VILLA ON THE HUDSON, NEAR WEEHAWKEN.

From this admirably chosen spot, the Bay of New York appears with every accessory of beauty. The city itself comes into the left of the picture to an advantage seen from no other point of view, the flocks of river-craft scud past in all directions, men-of-war, merchantmen, steamers, and ferry-boats, fill up the moving elements of the panorama; and far away beyond stretches the broad harbour, with its glassy or disturbed waters, in all the varieties of ever-changing sea-view. It was on this side that Hudson, who had felt the hostility of the Manhattan Indians, found a friendlier tribe, and made his first amicable visit on shore. The Indian tradition, springing from that visit,[2] and describing the first intoxication they had ever experienced, is extremely amusing.

"A long time ago, before men with a white skin had ever been seen, some Indians, fishing at a place where the sea widens, espied something at a distance moving upon the water. They hurried ashore, collected their neighbours, who together returned and viewed intensely this astonishing phenomenon. What it could be, baffled all conjecture. Some supposed it to be a large fish or animal, others that it was a very big house, floating on the sea. Perceiving it moving towards land, the spectators concluded that it would be proper to send runners in different directions to carry the news to their scattered chiefs, that they might send off for the immediate attendance of their warriors. These arriving in numbers to behold the sight, and perceiving that it was actually moving towards them (i.e. coming into the river or bay), they conjectured that it must be a remarkably large house, in which the Manitto (or Great Spirit), was coming to visit them. They were much afraid, and yet under no apprehension that the Great Spirit would injure them. They worshipped him. The chiefs now assembled at York Island, and consulted in what manner they should receive their Manitto: meat was prepared for a sacrifice; the women were directed to prepare the best of victuals; idols or images were examined and put in order; a grand dance they thought would be pleasing, and, in addition to the sacrifice, might appease him, if angry. The conjurers were also set to work, to determine what this phenomenon portended, and what the result would be. To these, men, women, and children, looked up for advice and protection. Utterly at a loss what to do, and distracted alternately by hope and fear, in this confusion a grand dance commenced. Meantime fresh runners arrived, declaring it to be a great house, of various colours, and full of living creatures. It now appeared certain that it was their Manitto, probably bringing some new kind of game. Others arriving, declared it positively to be full of people, of different colour and dress from theirs, and that one, in particular, appeared altogether red. This then must be the Manitto. They were lost in admiration; could not imagine what the vessel was, whence it came, or what all this portended. They are now hailed from the vessel in a language they could not understand; they answer by a shout or yell in their way. The house (or large canoe, as some render it) stops. A smaller canoe comes on shore, with the red man in it; some stay by his canoe, to guard it. The chiefs and wise men form a circle, into which the red man and two attendants approach. He salutes them with friendly countenance, and they return the salute after their manner. They are amazed at their colour and dress, particularly with him who, glittering in red, wore something (perhaps lace, or buttons) they could not comprehend. He must be the great Manitto, they thought; but why should he have a white skin? A large elegant hockhack (gourd, i.e. bottle, decanter, &c.) is brought by one of the supposed Manitto's servants, from which a substance is poured into a small cup or glass, and handed to the Manitto. He drinks, has the glass refilled, and handed to the chief near him; he takes it, smells it, and passes it to the next, who does the same. The glass in this manner is passed round the circle, and is about to be returned to the red-clothed man, when one of them, a great warrior, harangues them on the impropriety of returning the cup unempted. It was handed to them, he said, by the Manitto, to drink out of as he had; to follow his example would please him—to reject it might provoke his wrath; and if no one else would, he would drink it himself, let what would follow; for it was better for one even to die, than a whole nation to be destroyed. He then took the glass, smelled at it, again addressed them, bidding adieu, and drank the contents. All eyes were now fixed (on the first Indian in New York who had tasted the poison which has since affected so signal a revolution in the condition of the native Americans). He soon began to stagger; the women cried, supposing him in fits; he rolled on the ground; they bemoan his fate; they thought him dying. He fell asleep. They at first thought he had expired, but soon perceived he still breathed. He awoke, jumped up, and declared he never felt more happy; he asked for more; and the whole assembly imitating him, became intoxicated."

In descending the river, after he had penetrated to Albany, Hudson ran his little craft ashore at Weehawken; but the ground was a soft ooze, and she was got off without damage, and proceeded to sea.

[2]

It is disputed whether this scene of intoxication took place on the present site of New York, on the Jersey side, or at Albany.

VIEW OF MEREDITH, NEW HAMPSHIRE.

This beautiful town stands between the two lakes Winipiseogee and Sullivan and is deeply surrounded on every side with the most luxuriant rural beauty. The neighbourhood of these exquisite lakes, studded throughout with small green islands, burdened with foliage,—the lofty mountains, near and distant,—the fertility of the soil, and the healthiness of the spot, form a nucleus of attraction which gives Meredith great preference over other towns in New Hampshire. The Winipiseogee communicates, by the river of the same name, with the Merrimack River, and is near five hundred feet above the level of the sea.

This is the only part of New England, as far as we are aware, in which Indians were regularly hunted by parties who went out for the purpose, and received a bounty for their scalps. We have alluded elsewhere to Captain Lovewell, who surprised and killed a large party of sleeping Indians, and was killed himself afterwards, in the famous "Lovewell fight." The following tragedy, which took place on the Merrimack, in what was, in those days, the neighbourhood of Meredith, shows the provocation to this apparent inhumanity.

In the year 1697, a party of Indians, arrayed in their war dresses, approached the house of Mr. Dustan. This man was abroad at his usual labour. Upon the first alarm, he flew to the house, with a hope of hurrying to a place of safety his family, consisting of his wife, who had been confined a week only in child-bed; her nurse, a Mrs. Mary Jeff, a widow from the neighbourhood; and eight children. Seven of his children he ordered to flee, with the utmost expedition, in the course opposite to that in which the danger was approaching; and went himself to assist his wife. Before she could leave her bed, the savages were upon them. Her husband, despairing of rendering her any service, flew to the door, mounted his horse, and determined to snatch up the child with which he was unable to part, when he should overtake the little flock. When he came up to them, about two hundred yards from his house, he was unable to make a choice, or to leave any one of the number. He therefore determined to take his lot with them, and to defend them from their murderers, or die by their side. A body of the Indians pursued, and came up with him; and from near distances fired at him and his little company. He returned the fire, and retreated, alternately. For more than a mile he kept so resolute a face to his enemy, retiring in the rear of his charge, returned the fire of the savages so often, and with so good success, and sheltered so effectually his terrified companions, that he finally lodged them all safe from the pursuing butchers, in a distant house. When it is remembered how numerous his assailants were, how bold when an overmatch for their enemies, how active, and what excellent marksmen, a devout mind will consider the hand of Providence as unusually visible in the preservation of this family. Another party of the Indians entered the house, immediately after Mr. Dustan had quitted it, and found Mrs. Dustan, and her nurse, who was attempting to fly with the infant in her arms. Mrs. Dustan they ordered to rise instantly; and before she could completely dress herself, obliged her and her companion to quit the house, after they had plundered it and set it on fire. In company with several other captives, they began their march into the wilderness; she feeble, sick, terrified beyond measure, partially clad, one of her feet bare, and the season utterly unfit for comfortable travelling. The air was chilly and keen, and the earth covered, alternately, with snow and deep mud. Her conductors were unfeeling, insolent, and revengeful: murder was their glory, and torture their sport. Her infant was in her nurse's arms; and infants were the customary victims of savage barbarity. The company had proceeded but a short distance, when an Indian, thinking it an incumbrance, took the child out of the nurse's arms, and dashed its head against a tree. Such of the other captives as began to be weary, and lag, the Indians tomahawked. The slaughter was not an act of revenge or of cruelty; it was a mere convenience; an effort so familiar as not even to excite an emotion. Feeble as Mrs. Dustan was, both she and her nurse sustained, without yielding, the fatigue of the journey. Their intense distress for the death of the child, and of their companions, anxiety for those whom they had left behind, and unceasing terror for themselves, raised these unhappy women to such a degree of vigour, that notwithstanding their fatigue, their exposure to cold, their sufferance from hunger, and their sleeping on damp ground, under an inclement sky, they finished an expedition of about one hundred and fifty miles, without losing their spirits, or injuring their health. The weekwarm to which they were conducted, and which belonged to the savage who had claimed them as his property, was inhabited by twelve persons. In the month of April this family set out, with their captives, for an Indian settlement still more remote; and informed them, that when they arrived at the settlement, they must be stripped, scourged, and run the gauntlet, naked, between two files of Indians, containing the whole number found in the settlement; for such, they declared, was the standing custom of their nation. This information made a deep impression on the minds of the captive women, and led them irresistibly to devise all the possible means of escape. On the 31st of the same month, very early in the morning, Mrs. Dustan, while the Indians were asleep, having awaked her nurse, and a fellow-prisoner (a youth taken some time before, from Worcester), despatched, with the assistance of her companions, ten of the twelve Indians; the other two escaped. With the scalps of these savages, they returned through the wilderness; and, having arrived safely at Haverhill, and afterwards at Boston, received a handsome reward for their intrepid conduct, from the legislature."

BALLSTON SPRINGS.

These celebrated springs rise in a valley formed by a branch of the Kayaderosseras Creek. In this valley, and on its acclivities, is built the village called Ballston Spa. The medicinal character of the waters was discovered (as was said of Saratoga) by the beaten track of the deer to the springs at certain seasons. Ballston is now a populous village during the summer, and, since the rail-road has connected it with Saratoga, these two resorts have become like one, and, together, assemble, during certain months, the greater proportion of the moving population of the country. A description of the kind of life led at these springs accompanies another drawing in this Series.

At the time of the breaking out of the revolutionary war this part of the country was very thinly settled. The inhabitants for the most part took the continental side; but at the battle of Hoosac, a few miles from Ballston, a man was taken prisoner by the Americans, whose history exhibits some fine traits of character. He was a plain farmer from this neighbourhood, named Richard Jackson, and had conscientiously taken the British side in the contest. Feeling himself bound of course to employ himself in the service of his sovereign, he no sooner heard that Colonel Baum was advancing, than he saddled his horse and rode to Hoosac, intending to attach himself to this corps. Here he was taken, in such circumstances as proved his intention beyond every reasonable doubt. He was, besides, too honest to deny it. Accordingly he was transmitted to Great Barrington, then the shire-town of Berkshire, and placed in the hands of General Fellows, high sheriff of the county, who immediately confined him in the county gaol. This building was at that time so infirm, that without a guard no prisoner could be kept in it who wished to make his escape. To escape, however, was in no degree consonant with Richard's idea of right; and he thought no more seriously of making an attempt of this nature, than he would have done had he been in his own house. After he had lain quietly in gaol a few days, he told the sheriff that he was losing his time, and earning nothing, and wished that he would permit him to go out and work in the day time, promising to return regularly at evening to his quarters in the prison. The sheriff had become acquainted with his character, and readily acceded to his proposal. Accordingly Richard went out regularly during the remaining part of the autumn, and the following winter and spring, until the beginning of May, and every night returned at the proper hour to the gaol. In this manner he performed a day's work every day, with scarcely any exception beside the Sabbath, through the whole period.

In the month of May he was to be tried for high treason. The sheriff accordingly made preparations to conduct him to Springfield, where his trial was to be held; but he told the sheriff that it was not worth his while to take this trouble, for he could just as well go alone, and it would save both the expense and inconvenience of the sheriff's journey. The sheriff, after a little reflection, assented to his proposal, and Richard commenced his journey; the only one, it is believed, which was ever undertaken in the same manner for the same object. In the woods of Tyringham he was overtaken by the Hon. T. Edwards, from whom I had this story.—"Whither are you going?" said Mr. Edwards. "To Springfield, Sir," answered Richard, "to be tried for my life." Accordingly he proceeded directly to Springfield, surrendered himself to the sheriff of Hampshire, was tried, found guilty, and condemned to die.

The council of Massachusets was at this time the supreme executive of the State. Application was made to this board for a pardon. The facts were stated, the evidence by which they were supported, and the sentence grounded on them. The question was then put by the president, "Shall a pardon be granted to Richard Jackson?" The gentleman who spoke first observed that the case was perfectly clear; the act alleged against Jackson was unquestionably high treason; and the proof was complete. If a pardon should be granted in this case, he saw no reason why it should not be granted in every other. In the same manner answered those who followed him. When it came to the turn of Mr. Edwards, he told this story with those little circumstances of particularity, which, though they are easily lost from the memory, and have escaped mine, give light and shade, a living reality, and a picturesque impressiveness, to every tale which is fitted to enforce conviction, or to touch the heart. At the same time he recited it without enhancement, without expatiating, without any attempt to be pathetic. As is always the case, this simplicity gave the narration its full force. The council began to hesitate. One of the members at length observed— "Certainly such a man as this ought not to be sent to the gallows." To his opinion the members unanimously assented. A pardon was immediately made out and transmitted to Springfield, and Richard returned to his family.

Never was a stronger proof exhibited, that honesty is wisdom.

THE NARROWS, FROM FORT HAMILTON.

Not quite one hundred years after Verrazzano's discovery of the Bay of New York, during all which period we have no account of its having been visited by an European vessel, Hudson made the Capes of Virginia on his third cruise in search of the north-west passage. Standing still on a northward course, he arrived in sight of the Narrows, distinguishing from a great distance the Highlands of Never Sink, which his mate, Robert Juet, describes in the journal he kept as a "very good land to fall with, and a pleasant land to see."

The most interesting peculiarity of our country to a European observer, is the freshness of its early history, and the strong contrast it presents of most of the features of a highly civilized land, with the youth and recent adventure of a newly discovered one. The details of these first discoveries are becoming every day more interesting: and to accompany a drawing of the Narrows, or entrance to the Bay of New York, the most fit illustration is that part of the journal of the great navigator which relates to his first view of them. The following extracts describe the Narrows as they were two hundred years ago: the drawing presents them as they are.

"At three of the clock in the afternoone we came to three great rivers. So we stood along to the northernmost, thinking to have gone into it, but we found it to have a very shoald barre before it, for we had but ten foot water. Then we cast about to the southward, and found two fathoms, three fathoms, and three and a quarter, till we came to the souther side of them, then we had five or six fathoms, and anchored. So we sent in our boat to sound, and they found no less water than foure, five, six, and seven fathoms, and returned in an hour and a halfe. So we weighed and went in, and rode in five fathoms, ose ground, and saw many salmons, and mullets, and rayes very great.

"The fourth, in the morning, as soone as the day was light, we saw that it was good riding farther up. So we sent our boate to sound, and found that it was a very good harbour; then we weighed and went in with our ship. Then our boat went on land with our net to fish, and caught ten great mullets, of a foot and a half long apeece, and a ray as great as foure men could hale into the ship. So we trimmed our boat, and rode still all day. At night the wind blew hard at the north-west, and our anchor came home, and we drove on shore, but took no hurt, thanked bee God, for the ground is soft sand and ose. This day the people of the country came aboard of us, seeming very glad of our comming, and brought greene tobacco, and gave us of it for knives and beads. They go in deere skins loose, well dressed. They have yellow copper. They desire cloathes, and are very civill. They have great store of maise, or Indian wheate, whereof they make good bread. The country is full of great and tall oaks.

"The fifth, in the morning, as soone as the day was light, the wind ceased; so we sent our boate in to sound the bay. Our men went on land there and saw great store of men, women, and children, who gave them tobacco at their coming on land. So they went up into the woods, and saw great store of very goodly oakes, and some currants.

"The sixth, in the morning, was faire weather, and our master sent John Colman with foure other men in our boate over to the north side, to sound the other river," (the Narrows.) "They found very good riding for ships, and a narrow river to the westward," (probably what is now called the Kells, or the passage between Bergen-Neck and Staten Island,) "between two islands. The lands, they told us, were as pleasant, with grasse and flowers, and goodly trees, as ever they had seen, and very sweet smells came from them. So they went in two leagues and saw an open sea, and returned; and as they came backe they were set upon by two canoes, the one having twelve, the other fourteen men. The night came on, and it began to raine, so that their match went out; and they had one man slain in the fight, which was an Englishman, named John Colman, with an arrow shot into his throat, and two more hurt. It grew so dark that they could not find the shippe that night, but laboured to and fro on their oares.

"The seventh was fair, and they returned aboard the ship, and brought our dead man with them, whom we carried on land and buried."

On the eighth, Hudson lay still, to be more sure of the disposition of the natives before venturing farther in. Several came on board, but no disturbance occurred, and on the ninth he got under weigh, passed the Narrows, and proceeded by slow degrees up the river destined to bear his name.

THE NOTCH HOUSE—WHITE MOUNTAINS.

A considerable tract of land in New Hampshire was granted to two individuals of the names of Nash and Sawyer, for the discovery of "the Notch." This pass, the only one by which the inhabitants of a large extent of country, north-westward of these mountains, can, without a great circuit, make their way to the eastern shore, was known to the savages, who used to conduct their prisoners, taken on the coast, through this gap to Canada. By the people of New Hampshire, it was either unknown, or had been forgotten. Nash discovered it; but Sawyer persuaded Nash to admit him to an equal share of the benefits resulting from the discovery. It was, however, little advantage to either. They were both hunters, and with the thoughtlessness of men devoted to that employment, squandered the property soon after it was granted.

The Notch-house is inhabited by a family of the name of Crawford, who have the reputation, given them by travellers to the Notch, of being giants in size and strength. Ethan, one of the brothers living a mile or two further up, is called the "Keeper of the Mountains." A manuscript journal of a pedestrian excursion to Mount Washington lies before us, in which the writer (a friend of ours, who is a small Titan himself, and whose estimate of thewe and sinew is to be taken with a grain of allowance) rather sneers at the proportions of the mountain-keeper. After walking from thirty to thirty-four miles a day, mostly up hill, our friend and his companion arrive at the Notch-house.

"About one o'clock," says the journal, "we reached the house of T. G. Crawford, where we must remain till we can ascend Mount Washington. These Crawfords are not such giants as I had been led to suppose. We have not, however, seen Ethan, the most celebrated of the race.

"Last night we had a thunder shower, with sharp lightning. The thunder sounds heavy, and rumbles or echoes among the mountains with a very impressive effect. Just at evening we visited a beautiful cataract called the Flume, about half a mile from the house, and took the finest shower-bath I ever enjoyed. To-day the weather is doubtful, and we shall not attempt the ascent till to-morrow. There is enough in this immediate neighbourhood to occupy a week. The variety and magnificence of the scenery in every direction would satisfy the most ardent lover of the picturesque. Crawford is a fine fellow: his house is excellent, his trout delicious, and his neighbours perfectly quiet! The album kept here is an amusing omniana of nonsense and astonishment, sentiment and piety.

"After dinner walked over to Ethan Crawford's, and saw the celebrated 'Keeper of the White Mountains.' Expected to find him a giant, but were disappointed: he is a large man, and strong in muscle, but I have seen fifty larger and stronger in my own town. There is nothing remarkable in his manners or conversation. His voice is stentorian, and his style is marked by a rude bluntness and an apparent consciousness that something original is expected of him. On our return had a fine view of Mount Washington and his fellow-peaks. The monarch's head was capp'd with clouds, while all the others stood bare, as if uncovered for respect."

Another traveller thus speaks of the scenery of this spot:—"We rode six miles farther, and came to a farm occupied by a man named Crawford. Here the mountains assumed the form of an immense amphitheatre, elliptical in its figure, from twelve to fifteen miles in length, from two to four in breadth, and crowned with summits of vast height and amazing grandeur. Compared with this scene all human works of this nature, that of Titus particularly, so splendidly described by Gibbon, are diminished into toys and gewgaws. Here more millions could sit than hundreds there; every one of whom could look down with a full view on the valley beneath.

"The south-eastern extremity of this form was, some years since, the scene of a melancholy circumstance. A young woman, who had been employed at Jefferson, in the service of Colonel Whipple, had fallen deeply in love with a young man in the service of the same gentleman. At the close of autumn they agreed to go together to Portsmouth. On some occasion or other she was induced, before the time fixed for their departure, to go over to Lancaster. When she returned, she found him unexpectedly gone, and determined to follow him. December was already advanced, the snow had fallen deep, and there was not a house for thirty miles on the road. She set out on foot, and walked twenty-three miles from the house she had left, and then, overcome probably with fatigue, wrapped herself in her cloak, and lay down under a bush, where she was found a month afterwards, stiffened with frost."

WILKESBARRE—VALE OF WYOMING.

This beautiful town is situated on the eastern bank of the Susquehanna, opposite the village of Wyoming, celebrated in the "Gertrude" of Campbell. Like all the towns in this picturesque valley, it possesses fine points of picturesque beauty, and exhibits the thrift and agricultural prosperity which, all over the United States, contrast so strongly with the recent and unforgotten tales of the primitive wilderness.

There is a book, of which many copies do not now exist, entitled, "Observations made by John Bartram, in his Travels through Pennsylvania to the Lake Ontario," which presents a very wild picture of this part of the country in 1743. His companions were Mr. Weisar, a Mr. Evans, and a Delaware chief, called Shickalamy, and the object of their journey was to reconcile some differences between the English and the different Indian nations on that frontier. The dignity of their character as envoys from the English procured for them a kind reception, and the sight of many ceremonies not commonly seen by travellers. On their arrival on the banks of the Susquehanna, they were entertained by a hunting party of Indians, who served them up a roasted bear. Apropos to this, he describes the following superstition:—

"As soon as the bear is killed, the hunter places the small end of his pipe in its mouth, and, by blowing in the bowl, fills the mouth and throat full of smoke. He then conjures the departed spirit of the bear not to resent the injury done his body, nor to thwart his future sport in hunting. As he receives no answer to this, in order to know if his prayers have prevailed, he cuts the ligament under the bear's tongue. If these ligaments contract and shrivel up when cast into the fire, which is done with invocations and great solemnity, then it is esteemed a certain mark that the manes are appeased."

On the next day's journey, still following the winding bank of the east branch of the Susquehanna, they arrived at an Indian village, where the natives welcomed them by beating a rude drum. Assisting them to unsaddle their horses, they invited them into the principal wigwam, and cut long grass, and laid it on the floor for them to sit upon. The chiefs then came in with their pipes, (one of which, he says, was six feet long, with a stone head and a reed stem;) and immediately after they were regaled with roast venison, of which the morsel of honour was the neck, given to them for their share, to Mr. Bartram's great dissatisfaction. A superstitious ceremony took place here, the description of which is rather curious.

"They cut a parcel of poles, which they stick in the ground in a circle of about five feet diameter, and then bring them together at the top, and tie them in the form of an oven. In this the conjuror placeth himself, and his assistants cover his cage over with blankets. To make it still more suffocating, hot stones are rolled in. The conjuror then cries aloud, and agitates his body in the most violent manner; and when nature has lost almost all her faculties, the stubborn spirit becomes visible to him, generally in the shape of some bird. There is usually a stake driven into the ground about four feet high, and painted, for the airy visitant to perch upon while he reveals what the invocant wisheth to know. Sometimes there is a bowl of water, into which they often look when nearly exhausted, to see whether the spirit is ready to answer their demands."

The next day he encounters another superstition:—"On our left, as we journeyed, we perceived a hill, where the Indians told us that corn, tobacco, and squashes were found on the following occasion. An Indian of a distant tribe, whose wife had eloped, came hither to hunt, intending, with his skins, to purchase another wife. Coming to this hill, he espied a young squaw, sitting alone. Going to her and inquiring whence she came, she answered that she came from heaven to provide sustenance for poor Indians, and if he came to that place twelve months after, he should find food there. He came accordingly and found corn, squashes, and tobacco, which were propagated from thence, and spread through the country; and this silly story is religiously held for truth among them."

He kept on up the valley of the Susquehanna, through woods, where, as he describes it, "the tops of the trees for miles together were so close to one another that there is no seeing which way the clouds drive, nor knowing which way the wind sets; and it seems as if the sun had never shone on the ground beneath since the creation." It is a description of a complete wilderness, till he reaches the borders of Lake Ontario—a tract of country that, in ninety years from the time he wrote, is seamed with rail-roads and canals, and teeming with towns, improvement and speculation.

SQUAWM LAKE.

The Indianesque, but not very pretty name, in which this lovely body of waters rejoices, has been once or twice changed, but the force of usage has uniformly triumphed. Dr. Dwight called it Sullivan's Lake, after Major-General Sullivan, formerly governor of

85

the State; and the adjoining waters of Winipiseogee, he named Lake Wentworth, after another governor; but both have fallen into disuse, and the original names have reverted.

The great defect in American Lakes, generally, is the vast, unrelieved expanse of water, without islands and promontories, producing a fatigue on the eye similar to that of the sea. Squawm and Winipiseogee Lakes are exceptions to this observation. They are connected by so narrow an isthmus that five hundred dollars, it is said, would pay the expense of uniting them: and their islands together amount, it is said also, to exactly three hundred and sixty-five. As this singular coincidence has been remarked of several other lakes, however, the assertion seems rather apocryphal.

Some of the very loveliest scenery in the world lies about these two lakes, yet they are seldom visited. The country around is fertile, and sufficiently cultivated to soften the appearance of wilderness, which it might receive from the prevalency of forest, and the luxuriance of vegetation; but the mountains, which form its back-ground from every point, shutting it in like an amphitheatre, seem to seclude it from the flow of population.

Nature is a capricious beauty, and, like most other beauties, has her best looks, and her favourable times, to be seen to advantage. Beautiful as she is at Squawm Lake in the first plenitude of spring, she is more beautiful in the first flush over her face of the bright colours of autumn. The autumnal tints of our forests are peculiar to America, but there are some parts of the country where, for various reasons, this phenomenon is much more beautiful than at others. The moisture of the land about these lakes, the extreme luxuriance of the sap in consequence, and the liability of the whole of this region to sudden changes of temperature, contribute to its brilliancy. The sharp frost of a single night effects a change very often that seems almost miraculous, and the multiplication of these gawdy colours in the mirror of the surrounding waters, the bright golden, crimson, and purple islands, and the gorgeous hill-sides, all reflected and redoubled, make it a scene which the imagination never could pre-conceive. From a late publication we extract a description of this phenomenon, made from observation, and finished with some care.

"The first severe frost had come, and the miraculous change had passed upon the leaves which is known only in America. The blood-red sugar maple, with a leaf brighter and more delicate than a Circassian lip, stood here and there in the forest like the sultan's standard in a host—the solitary and far-seen aristocrat of the wilderness; the birch, with its spirit-like and amber leaves, ghosts of the departed summer, turned out along the edges of the woods like a lining of the palest gold; the broad sycamore and the fan-like catalpa flaunted their saffron foliage in the sun, spotted with gold like the wings of a lady-bird; the kingly oak, with its summit shaken bare, still hid its majestic trunk in a drapery of sumptuous dyes, like a stricken monarch, gathering his robes of state about him, to die royally in his purple; the tall poplar, with its minaret of silver leaves, stood blanched like a coward in the dying forest, burthening every breeze with its complainings; the hickory paled through its enduring green; the bright berries of the mountain-ash, flushed with a more sanguine glory in the unobstructed sun; the gaudy tulip-tree, the sybarite of vegetation, stripped of its golden cups, still drank the intoxicating light of noon-day in leaves than which the lip of an Indian shell was never more delicately tinted; the still deeper-dyed vines of the lavish wilderness, perishing with the noble things whose summer they had shared, outshone them in their decline, as woman in her death is heavenlier than the being on whom in life she leaned; and alone and unsympathizing in this universal decay, outlaws from nature, stood the fir and the hemlock; their frowning and sombre heads darker and less lovely than ever, in contrast with the death-struck glory of their companions.

"The dull colours of English autumnal foliage give you no conception of this marvellous phenomenon. The change here is gradual; in America it is the work of a night—of a single frost!

"Oh, to have seen the sun set on hills bright in the still green and lingering summer, and to awake in the morning to a spectacle like this!

"It is as if a myriad of rainbows were laced through the tree-tops—as if the sunsets of a summer—gold, purple, and crimson—had been fused in the alembic of the west, and poured back in a new deluge of light and colour over the wilderness. It is as if every leaf in these countless trees had been painted to outflush the tulip—as if, by some electric miracle, the dyes of the earth's heart had struck upward, and her crystals and ores, her sapphires, hyacinths, and rubies, had let forth their imprisoned colours to mount through the roots of the forests, and, like the angels that in olden time entered the bodies of the dying, re-animate the perishing leaves, and revel an hour in their bravery."

SABBATH-DAY POINT, LAKE GEORGE.

The lovely waters of Lake George are known to the Catholics by the prettier and more appropriate name of Lake Sacrament. Its singular transparency, surpassing that of all other lakes in the world, probably suggested some tradition of its sacredness; and its water was carried to great distances to supply the consecrated fonts. The singular seclusion of its position, far aside from the general current of population, has assisted to preserve its character.

Loch Katrine, at the Trosachs, is a miniature-likeness of Lake George. It is the only lake in Europe that has at all the same style or degree of beauty. The small green islands, with their abrupt shores,—the emerald depths of the water, overshadowed and tinted by the tenderest moss and foliage,—the lofty mountains in the back-ground,—and the tranquil character of the lake, over which the wind is arrested and rendered powerless by the peaks of the hills and the lofty island-summits,—are all points of singular resemblance. Loch Katrine can scarce be called picturesque, except at the Trosachs, however; while Lake George, throughout all the mazes of its three hundred and sixty-five islands (there are said to be just this number), preserves the same wild and racy character of beauty. Varying in size, from a mile in length to the circumference of a tea-table, these little islets present the most multiplied changes of surface and aspect—upon some only moss and flowers, upon others a miniature forest, with its outer trees leaning over to the pellucid bosom of the lake, as if drawn downwards by the reflection of their own luxuriant beauty.

The forests on the shores of Lake George were formerly stocked plentifully with deer, who were hunted in rather a peculiar manner. The huntsmen were divided into two parties, one of which started them from their thickets on the edge of the lake. Upon hearing the approach of the dogs, they invariably took to the water and crossed to the opposite shore, from which a boat, directed by a boy stationed in a high tree, put out to meet them. A few blows with an oar conquered them easily, and they were towed ashore, or taken alive into the boat. Bears are hunted in the same manner, except that, being more inconvenient to close with, they are usually shot from the boat without ceremony.

The race of settlers who were to be found in these neighbourhoods not many years ago—half hunters, half farmers—has disappeared, or gone westward with the game. The celebrated theologian, Dr. Dwight, gives a graphic account of one of this class, whom he met in a first visit to Lake George, somewhere about the year 1800. Landing on a point to dine, in his passage up the lake, he found a huntsman, with a buck lying beside him. "Before our departure," he says, "we heard the hounds advancing near to us. Our new companion instantly took fire at the sound. His eye kindled; his voice assumed a loftier tone; his stride became haughty; his style swelled into pomp, and his sentiments were changed rapidly from mildness to ardour, to vehemence, and to rage. I was forcibly struck with the sameness of the emotions produced by hunting and by war. The ardour of battle, the glitter of arms, and the shock of conflict, could scarcely have produced in a single moment more violent or fierce agitations than were roused in this man by the approach of the hounds, the confident expectation of a victim, and the brilliant prospect of a venatory triumph. To him who has been a witness of both objects, it will cease to be a wonder that the savage should make the chase a substitute for war, and a source of glory second only to that acquired in battle. Our hunter was not exempted, however, from the common lot of man. His partner came up with the hounds, but without a deer! The magnificence of our companion dwindled in a moment. The fire vanished from his eye; his voice fell to its natural key; and the hero shrank into a plain farmer."

No one, it has been well said, understands the character of the aboriginal tenants of America, who has seen them only as vitiated by contact with the settlers. I say vitiated; for, if they are not made better by proper protection and cultivation, they become much worse; as human nature, left to itself, is more susceptible of the contagion of vice, than of improvement in virtue. The Indian, thrown into temptation, easily takes the vices of the white man; and, in such exposure, his race melts away like the snow before a summer's sun.

The wild Indian, however, whose contact with the European race has not been enough to vitiate his habits, or subdue his self-importance—who still prowls the forest in the pride of his independence—who looks upon all nations and tribes, but his own, as unworthy of the contemptuous glance of his eye—whose dreams of importance become to him a constant reality, and actually have the same influence in the formation of his character as if they were all they seem to him—he regards himself as the centre of a world made purposely for him. Such a being (and the wild Indian is much more than this) who is not a creature of the imagination, but a living actor in the scenes of the earth, becomes at least an interesting object, if not, also, a problem yet to be solved in both moral philosophy and politics, and in the nature and character of man as a social being. His bearing may be imagined from the following description of the war-dance:—

"A hundred warriors now advance,
All dressed and painted for the dance;
And sounding club and hollow skin,
A slow and measured time begin.
With rigid limb and sliding foot,
And murmurs low the time to suit,
For ever varying with the sound,
The circling band moves round and round.
Now slowly rise the swelling notes,
And every crest more lively floats.
Now tossed on high with gesture proud
Then lowly 'mid the circle bowed;
While clanging arms grow louder still,
And every voice becomes more shrill,
Till fierce and strong the clamour grows,
And the wild war-whoop bids it close,
Then starts Skuntonga forth, whose band
Came far from Huron's storm-beat strand,

And loud recounts his hunting feats,
Whilst his dark club the measure beats."—Ontwa.

Sabbath-day Point presents one of the most beautiful of the many views upon the lake. It received its name from Lord Amherst, who landed there with his suite to breakfast on a Sunday morning. It is about twenty-five miles from the head of the lake.

END OF VOL. I.

Printed in the USA
CPSIA information can be obtained
at www.ICGtesting.com
LVHW022251270923
759569LV00010B/352

9 781530 925643